MORE STORIES

MORE STORIES

T P NASH

Troubador Publishing Ltd
Unit E2 Airfield Business Park,
Harrison Road, Market Harborough,
Leicestershire LE16 7UL
Tel: 0116 279 2299
Email: books@troubador.co.uk
Web: www.troubador.co.uk

ISBN 978-1-83628-080-4

British Library Cataloguing in Publication Data.
A catalogue record for this book is available from the British Library.

Printed and bound in Great Britain by 4edge Limited
Typeset in 11pt Garamond Pro by Troubador Publishing Ltd, Leicester, UK

For Sarah

Contents

Contents

The Ambassadors

He cursed as pigment spilled onto the floor and glanced down; his best hose, immaculate, thank goodness. What was he doing here?

With a groan, he knelt down and brushed it up. He hated mess. At home, servants cleaned floors. And clothes. And mixed paint for him. What a bore. Here, he was required to be a slave as well as an apprentice. Not that he felt he had much to learn; he had just spent two years in the Medici household. What better education could he possibly have had? He was not too concerned with the techniques of painting but more interested in learning the business of art: the wooing of potential clients, the placing of works of art in the right hands at a good profit, being in the right place at the right time. Caught in the egoism of youth, he saw no obstruction to his plans, to the creation of his world. At a different time and in a different place it might not have been so easy but he came from the centre of the cultured world.

On his knees, he looked at the empty room. The floor stretched away from him as large as a tennis court, the oak shining in the morning sun with the warm smell of beeswax. He imagined the King playing tennis; he was so stout he could hardly bend. No Tuscan would stoop to such indignity.

The walls were hung with Flemish tapestries, hunting and classical scenes, and there were three tall casement windows set in deep reveals on one side. Dust floated in the sunshine. The room was grand, designed to impress the impressionable, persuade the powerful, but Andrea looked at the old-fashioned ceiling and the heavy oak furniture. Bah, architecture was so backward here. And those tapestries. They reminded him of those in the Palazzo Signoria; faded colours, hanging threads. So old, so old-fashioned.

There was a deep silence that resonated with unspoken secrets and unseen threats. Where were the courtiers, where was the life in this vast Palace? At times since he had come to England, though he would not admit it, he could not help feeling a little insecure, on the point of a stiletto. He did not know enough about the English. Who were they, these barbaric Northerners? Could he be made to disappear on the whim of some official, accused of spying and never see the light of day again? He knew it happened in his own State, the most civilized in the world.

His passport came with letters of introduction to seek banking links between the City of London and his father's bank in Verona. He hated banking but he had not dared to tell his father; the banks were full of boring boys, who talked only of money and profit and knew nothing of painting or culture. They were scarcely gentlemen. He would marry into a fortune, move in aristocratic circles and deal in fashionable paintings, so much more lucrative than manufacturing paintings himself. Or banking. His Florentine background with Medici connections would ensure success. In the meantime, he would serve out his time apprenticed to his father and learn the business of painting. And accumulate a small fund of ducats and a large number of valuable connections.

The door opened. A maid came in and stopped, hand to her mouth. Andrea made his most gallant bow. The maid blushed, staring at him. He laughed and strode over to her. Would she be suitable for an evening's entertainment, he wondered. These English girls, when one had stripped them of their shyness, weren't they the same as girls all over the world?

His master came into the room. The girl vanished.

'Confound it. The King commands me to paint a three-quarter portrait of the French Ambassador and the French Ambassador commands me to paint a full length portrait, and, by the way, include his friend who is visiting.'

'An important work, Signor.'

'Important? It will be three times as much work for no more money and I have no choice. The life of a Court painter! Huh.'

He stood in a silence at his easel in a shaft of strong sunlight. Andrea dared not speak. The life of a Court painter? No lack of commissions, however onerous. A few warm beds and a life of comfort; there must be worse ways to earn a living. He returned to the table, mixing umber for the cartoon, laying out chalk and mahl sticks and wondering how far the composition had moved forward in his master's mind.

The Ambassador and his friend entered. As Andrea and his master made deep bows, he looked up at the Frenchmen; the Ambassador looked like the King, short and square but more friendly. His friend was younger, with an arrogant sneer.

'Ah, Holbein, there you are,' said the Ambassador. 'Shall we make a start? Where do you want us?'

He chatted to Holbein in English and French, about pictures and countries; Andrea struggled to understand, wishing he had paid more attention to his tutor. The other man did not join in the conversation but beckoned to Andrea.

'Wine and sweetmeats. What are you waiting for?'

Andrea looked at his master; did he have to go running around for these Frenchmen? He was there to be an artist, to assist his master. Who gave him a nod and sent him to find a palace servant.

When he returned, they were discussing the science of navigation. The Ambassador was a ship-owner; he suggested that the picture should incorporate instruments for navigation, in addition to the musical instruments to show that he was a man of the arts, and holy books to show that he was a good follower of the Church, the One Holy Catholic Church. Not, thought Andrea, the Church that he had heard mentioned in London: a Church of England. He hoped that nobody was spying on them; at home, the Duke would have at least two concealed men behind the tapestries or in the window reveals or even under floors in some places.

Eventually, Holbein persuaded the sitters to take up position; he had much to do as the Ambassador told him that another sitting would not be possible for the friend, the Bishop de Selve; the Bishop would be returning to France shortly. Andrea wondered what business brought him to England, a Catholic Bishop in this country. Perhaps the Pope had entrusted him with the job of reining in King Henry. Not much chance of that from what he had heard. Or perhaps he was spying for the King of France.

The work proceeded slowly. The Bishop wandered off occasionally to gaze out of the window; Andrea noticed his master becoming impatient as he repositioned his arm, yet again. De Dinteville, the Ambassador, was more co-operative. He asked if Holbein had explored perspective; surely, it was a fabrication was it not, some trickery? The architect

Alberti had designed it. Did he know of Mantegna's Christ? Extraordinary! Andrea listened; he was interested in the science of perspective and had learned a great deal in Florence. But he was careful to keep his ideas to himself; the religious authorities did not care for any science that challenged the word of God. He knew that Holbein would not commit himself; he had fled the Reformation in Europe and Andrea never spoke of religion with him.

'And what of you, young man?' The Ambassador caught Andrea off guard.

'Signor, I am only a student of painting from Tuscany.' Andrea was glad that he had dressed well; he liked to make a good impression with persons of power. You never knew ...

'Si, you have a Florentine accent, do you not?' De Dinteville looked at him closely.

'Signor, I was brought up in Verona but my father sent me to the Medici family to learn banking. And once there I learnt painting.'

'Well, you are a lucky young man in an interesting time. But are you a banker or a painter? I wonder. Come and see me some time. I may be able to introduce you to some French painters.' And he laughed, a light tinkling sound without warmth.

Andrea resisted the temptation to make some disparaging comment about French art; what he had seen was of poor quality, antiquated and dull.

'Well, master painter, how much longer do you

need us?' said De Dinteville. 'You have an interesting apprentice; beware, he may compete for your commissions.'

'If I could just have a few more minutes, Your Excellency ...'

De Dinteville and his friend stood in silence for the next ten minutes. Then Holbein brushed down the chalk dust from his apron and bowed deeply to his sitters. De Selve left the room at once while de Dinteville looked at the cartoon and congratulated Holbein on his draughtsmanship.

'Don't forget what we discussed, master painter.' He wandered out of the room.

Andrea wondered what the Ambassador had meant. Holbein sighed.

'Whatever country you work in, young Andrea, the powerful are always the same. Well mannered or foul, they want everything their own way. I shall sup early; I'm tired.'

They summoned their boy, who collected the easel, pigments and chalks, and left the Palace.

In the studio, Andrea assembled the scene for the Ambassador's painting: a heavy green curtain, brocaded and pleated, hung to absorb the light and show the flesh tints to good effect and a tall table with a small Oriental rug laid over it. At his master's direction, he painted a pattern on the floor, like the paving in front of the high altar in Westminster

Abbey. He recognised the trust placed in him; the pattern emphasised the perspective of the design, leading the eye into the picture. He placed stands in the sitters' positions to hold the clothes that had been borrowed and scraped the oak boards that his master would paint on, filling and rubbing, laying down a ground to seal the surface.

As Holbein painted, Andrea ground pigment, mixed paint, tested colours, and watched. He was allowed to assist in pricking through the cartoon to transfer the drawing onto the boards and draw a perspective of the floor. He had to assemble the instruments, both musical and scientific: a torquetum for calculating the course of a ship, a quadrant, globes, an odd sundial, and a number of books, religious items. He was accustomed to paintings showing symbolic references of piety but a number of the scientific instruments were unknown to him.

'They are new to you? Do your people not understand the sciences and mathematics and how the heavens work?' said Holbein.

Andrea did not know what to say. His Church limited knowledge and scientific exploration and he knew of young artists who had disappeared after carrying out dissections of dead bodies. During his journey to England, he saw that scientific knowledge was advancing in other countries and accumulated as much knowledge as he could. He did not like to admit his ignorance but believed that he could still impress his master with the one science in which the Italians had always excelled.

There was a skull with the other instruments. Holbein was having difficulty finding a place for it; he picked it up and put it down, again and again. Andrea knew that it was an important emblem though lately unfashionable. He asked him why it must be included.

'Do you not see? I must suggest the discord between riches and religion, and man's knowledge of the world and science. I must also show the meaninglessness of earthly life and the certainty of mortality. But I have a further problem; the Ambassador does not wish to have a skull. He says that in his country such symbols are becoming less visible, whatever he means by that. It is too important to leave out and I don't know how to depict it.'

Andrea smiled. 'Signor, I believe that there is a way to show things that are not there.'

'What do you mean? Are you wasting my time, Andrea? You know I must represent the Ambassador so that he will be admired. And keep him happy. What on earth are you talking about?'

Andrea bowed, unable to meet his master's eyes. He coughed.

'But Signor, would you permit me, please? You can show the skull so that it will not interfere with the sitters. And then you will have included it, as an image of mystery, an image seen only from one point.'

'Mystery? Is this some devilish device you are proposing? Andrea, we do not have time for such nonsense. Perhaps you had better -'

'Oh no, master. If you permit me, I could draw a few views for you.'

There was a long pause; Andrea felt Holbein looking down on him. He stared at the floor. Holbein cleared his throat.

'Very well. For the present, we shall continue with the painting. But you had better do well or I shall look for another apprentice.'

Holbein painted and Andrea assisted, avoiding discussions and doing everything he could to please his master. He mixed paints, moved objects, hung garments, painted undercoats and, when he had time, prepared a folio of drawings. He wanted to prove himself; he was determined to persuade his master to adopt something unusual, to show these ignorant Englishmen that they also had so much to learn.

One afternoon, he was summoned and told to lay his folio open. Holbein spent time examining each view, spreading them around him. He frowned and asked questions.

'Is this accurate?' 'Where is the skull in this one?' 'What are you up to here?' 'Where would I put this one?' 'What is this?'

Andrea gave answers as best as he could, not daring to upset him. Time passed. Holbein stood up.

'Very well, Andrea. I knew all these things were

possible but I did not believe that they would be useful to me. You have impressed me. Now, which one do you think I should choose?'

'Master, this one. If the King will not like it, could you not persuade him that it promotes discourse, an image that will be remembered?'

'Have you tried persuading the King of anything?'

'But signor, you could always tell him that you knew the painting would be hung high and that the image is better seen from below, as one approaches.'

'I should string you from the rafters for your impudence. Very well, I shall paint that odd view of yours. May it not bring the wrath of the King upon my head. Perhaps I shall leave it to you to present the painting to Court ...'

The painting was finished. Andrea would have liked to hear how the Court received the painting but he was already returning to Florence to his new business, a school for artists.

School Days

Sun cutting across the roofs deep shadows yet and slumbers all around I sigh tracing the line of escape over the Quad past Manual lifting above Armoury to the glowing roof of Donachers to fly off into the morning air losing 1 degree Fahrenheit with every 300 feet elevation old Grimmers said as I soar free of eternal History essays; my history a puzzled past with parents pattering on about their own illustrious pasts, I must do well Pater, must do well must I not to equal all that you have done, but could I not soar free and choose a life without harrowing expectations ...

I think of her ...

A shuddering sighing cough racks the corridor. It's too early, leave me alone to wonder the infinite gifts of life and be out of this containing world, narrow walls of study a slot in my life, too early for fag to clean my shoes fetch my towel make tea and beg for time off lazy sod can't treat him badly like others do, I lean out of the window was it not this very window that my brother stretched his bull's pestle to make a walking stick in one summer term warm humid air stretch it with weights dangling clear topped with an appropriate knob where is it now …

Dear Ozzy does he sleep still shall I run to his House disturb his slumbers I would be not alone take him by the scruff and dive deep in the Pool to rise bubbling in shouted freedom before it all must stop. Osborne known him since Prep parents Services some far flung RAF station could it be Cyprus or Kenya we met a rough tussle a challenge neither stepping down I hardly recall some small thing but recognized each other from aeons before like dogs that run together …

We ran side by side through years and teams and exams and Houses to be here, where will he be in a twelvemonth I don't know he'll not make the Cambridge exam that I must sit poor beggar … that's both of us.

I told him of her.

A cat stalks diagonally across the Quad, kitchens to Biology Lab lump of meat in mouth perhaps to feed a brood the Biology cat nurtured by the master old Peddar mad old hatter odd bod at the best of times thank goodness I don't do Biology all stretched frog skins and putrid stink preservative leaking through grey suits staining ties only the Sixth have tunics white once but now impossible fluorescent stains yellows and acrid reds Peddar his stinking pipe shields him though he hacks from morning to night …

Morning looms I write a dozen words or two to satisfy the itch a question that has to be investigated have I learnt enough read enough to know how to make a brave break pursue the radical question that will have my good Master twist his hands in glee – or pain – and ask the harder question back had I considered that had I boy? Will you be ready to sit the paper only a matter of weeks must brush up on the eighteenth Century not quite there I think what do you think boy do you think at all? But Sir … but Sir gets me nowhere it must be sound argument in my haste I have it yes surely George II was not the fool his father thought as he banished him from Court I believe it can I convince with this script this weekly essay?

The briefest of washes cold splashing on privates scratch the old back itch gurning to brush the teeth back to the room pulling on the old clothes then wrapped in black gown – if only trimmed in ermine like some Doctorate – stamp down the stairs for Breakfast boy get out of my way yes you are late report to me no I don't know when just later old stained wainscoting scraped with decades centuries of passing bodies here and there scratched initials some a hundred years old like the ones on the benches in the Chapel was their life so different some think more violent some think drinking in the studies fags warming their boots and perhaps their beds cold nights it still goes on Saturday nights in the big dorms never happened with me though I recall the odd groan some boy relieving himself can't say I blamed him Rector lectured us frequently on sins of lust all the old things brought smiles to many ...

Shall I skip Chapel to finish my essay blast no on duty report the late-comers a strike or two for the cheeky Third Formers slipper or cane Prefects' choice ...

Diningroom echoes to decades of boys at the trough high piping voices small boys scatter like minnows before respected elders I am one old framed Heads look down on us some famous names chemists and politics what do they think of us – if they could – the young'uns skip I shall have them skip to bring me porridge and toast and marmalade no bacon for me can't bear the fat so early greasy rashers hung out on forks little boys shriek to avoid the flying fat a sudden Silence he said ...

House Master strides among us Silence boy twists the ear of some nicompoop in the Second some problem of a flooded Bathroom is it in my duty no thank goodness Bates or Sampson they'll hear of it he passes me by a nod all goes well with you good good and swinging gown draughts on its way door banging and clamour climbs I'm out of there ...

No time until Chapel except for a crap and a whistle while I ponder my essay is it good enough then I think of her to take me through the minutes left where is she now breakfast at her school I wonder and will she be baring for hockey or gym? Does she think of me as I pore over her letters weekly they come a pink envelope if lucky makes chaps jealous to see my pleasure. Girls together do they laugh at each other catty no doubt longing for hols exams first the same as mine though somehow different …

Never had a peep of her all all in the imagination dare not put it in my letters though she bares her heart to me a silent longing scented in the fibres of the paper almost always a lipstick kiss to sign off and no lipstick allowed at her school …

We stand together to sing the old hymns shouting out words we choose Rector pontificates prayers endless it seems the Head sighs aloud looking over the ranks of grey suits black ties grey shirts white for the older boys Masters avoid his eye does he give them grief do they return home in the evening to the loving ear of wives with awful tales of his doings? Some Masters have no wives are they in training for it or not allowed to scratch that itch some have to live in House appear the very properness celibate it's called due to young gentlemen who are to carry the School's name out into the world – oh look there's a young man from the School how well he looks … or otherwise …

Now we mix with day boys fresh from their homes over the County a separate breed nice some of them I have visited a house here and there been received by well-meaning mums swam in rivers and pools open to the sky chatted to sisters some of whom are schooled across the Park one has been out to secret trysts among

the arboreta swapped notes kisses forbidden touches –
she is far away so far away …

Ancient Chapel echoes our final prayers then
shuffling disorderly exit avoiding some Masters the
Head leads off we pass him outside in conference with
a Master one may be summoned eyes down slide past
the other side speed to the Study collect this morning's
books English first a free period and then the History
man yes the essay one free period to polish rewrite if
time allows …

In the Quad warm air hovers would be good to be
on the farm at home stubble still standing from harvest
a quiet time harrowing already to prepare the seedbeds
for cereals be told the sugarbeet bodes well the income
my next term's fees he says – every time – pass on to
the English room and here is Ozzy our own greeting
important to absolutely ignore each other until we
collide in a doorway the tussle as at the beginning of us
we welcome the day together stand as heroes a match
this afternoon or training for the Fifteen a friendly
shove off to our desks always the same ones that's the
way Frenchy likes it helps to remember our names
he said as though he hasn't been teaching us this six
years the sun roasting through the windows dust motes
the odd cough a yawn not mine English proceeds he
is aware of those preparing for Cambridge the local
University a gentle but firm line makes me nervous he
pulls out old papers forecasts the subjects most likely
no promises a smile a wink directs us to Hardy and

Donne no sweat you must be joking I think recall that we have seen it Michaelmas term I think it was time passes writing a sonnet to my beloved ringing it with roses I'll send it to her next …

A nub of chalk strikes my forehead with percussive force …

The note is in his hand some sarcastic comment perhaps I should be employed writing Greeting Cards a worthwhile job eh I grimace crawl quote Donne dare a quip on my sonnet he screws it up tosses in the wpb I'll recover it later the bell goes I'm in my Study tempted to rewrite my love note – I recovered it while some boy distracted him with an asinine question – my love is like an itch that must be scratched how long to wait now until the holidays then to fly with ardour over Counties to her haunt will she be as pleased impatient to see me I grind my nose to my essay sweat it a blackbird lands on the cill to peck at crumbs put out daily lifted from breakfast white sliced but am I deceiving myself George II I must be right deceive my Master with original thought my God that must be a first I scrawl a few lines of erudition …

I'm on the way …

Deep in his chair in thought we are unseen we jiffle nervous a few whispered words have you finished your essay did you read the Oxford History awfully good blast I had not thought it like a sudden wind he rises and gazing out of the window a weary sigh calls my name if you please sir would you read the first page of your essay for our general elucidation I hesitate I take it you have finished the essay set only last week or are you too busy with Sports or other wasting occupations is not the Entrance exam in four no three weeks? Stand up if you please so all may hear your … I read not fast so that the argument may appear like neon to my fellows Master will see through it I know he interrupts did not George I ban his son from Court though he held to his grandchildren how does this affect your argument I speak too hasty he says you must assemble thoughts in your head before uttering how would you fare in an Interview worse a Viva I stop flush tie too tight start again he listens in silence that is a change asks for the Summary please where is your argument going and at the end he laughs Young sir you could charm the skin off a cod fillet but I doubt the Fellows at Cambridge will be so easily convinced and yet you have an idea not to be so speedily dismissed I wish you had researched a little further yes why don't you in addition to next week's essay expand this one because you must admit it is a little on the light side is it not? He laughs again not unpleasant and calls on someone else I sit back Ozzy is not in this class a Languages man I wonder how he is faring I think of her …

A sharp slap of the cane upon my desk …

Perhaps young sir you could elaborate on the question we were discussing I risk an answer he groans make sure your George II essay is very good class continues to break I groan and ache with all the concentration the heat the itch then a packet of crisps instant coffee in the House Prefects Room a few words with Ozzy see you later and it's in to Geography …

Lunch a roaring assault on ears and arms boys all crowded together shouting laughter then done the Fifteen assembles an inspirational word some strategies I should not be there five times round the field to loosen desk-bound muscles Ozzy has not appeared chaps from his House saw him at lunch could not be sure perhaps he has work to do often behind A levels again next summer not Cambridge entrance nor some redbrick institution I ask after him send good wishes bid them treat him well …

Days pass …

The work a mountain to be climbed sometimes I am as Sisyphus as essays are returned for rewriting amending refining until I could gag but slowly it sinks in I have no Fifteen no Ozzy I don't have time to watch matches nor think of my weekly letters though I receive hers still guilty I am she must know I have to work until the blood runs from beneath my nails and what is worse …

Ozzy is ill …

They do not know he has been taken home I miss his chunter his company after exams I will visit him bring him news of School see his sister a good sort young we'll have a good time play games tennis wander down to the village pub I miss him bend to my work go through Geography again specialize in Water and

Ice they speak of history of geography English is the hardest so personal I have to know my books Donne is hard some say easy and History I would read at University if I get there dreaming of spires no that's the other place …

Exams arrive sealed envelopes bearing my future Masters convey them in locked briefcases strange looks from English and History what do they know a little pitying some hopeful smiles words of encouragement I am a machine programmed with information and primed with ideas for the start pen filled pencils sharpened no thoughts of others or sports or … honed myself as a weapon to slice through the week of exams no thought of others it passes in a blur in the exam room to drag out minute by minute between, the papers are collected sealed no comment from Masters a few discussions with fellows but I like to step away breathe fresh air until the next …

At the end to return to my indolent self to dream …

Passed a pink envelope I missed them this last few weeks smiling rip it open and shortly gulp a stagger she has thrown me over you have not written recently why have you treated me like that I loved you I shall be away the summer hols it is better to have a complete break she does not return the ring I gave her one hot evening Goodbye and good …

Does it hurt I'm not sure but it is not right I shrug to let it go …

Ozzy is not seen I glean little information it must be serious why can they not tell I see his Housemaster – my Geog teacher – a palliative word not to worry catch up with him in the hols look forward to your results and University eh? Sure to have done well and what have you planned for the Summer …

I see Ozzy next a glimpse between others at a cricket match he seems to have faded to a wraith was a little distant I give him time to catch up catch glimpses of him here and there or think I do give encouraging glances words of friendship not returned days pass I miss our closeness …

the last day of Term the last day of School forever only results to follow in the hols he is walking across the Quad as though never absent I tell him of exams girl lost matches how I missed our casual chat …

he stares at me his face blank humour in his eyes though but it may be the sun reflecting off the Physics block I am blinded turn away he is there on the other side of me …

Bows his head seemed to say he couldn't find him on the other side it may be too early where did you go? I say the usual place? Is it still standing? He gives an odd look shakes his head something about the old place I can't be sure …

By the Manual a crowd of boys surround us stare at me pass on …

and he is no longer there …

After class my last and a new world looming I cannot guess at the shape of it I left my Form to walk ahead and he is there beside me as before I say you know what you were talking about …

He shudders looks awfully thin and seems to want me to understand to catch up to be with him …

I didn't know what to make of this coughed looking around he is not himself I am confused come on old chap shall we go down to the Greyhound …

He looks over his shoulder at me suddenly I stagger with an immense feeling of grief the loneliness of loss briefly there is a shy smile like the old Ozzy a wave to summon me to the other side …

I was frozen in a vacuum pierced by no sound or movement.

Royal Albert Bridge, Saltash. Elevation of Cornish Truss, 1 September 1857.

As Fisher took in the tea, Brunel stirred in his cot.

'Time? Weather? Location?'

'Sir, it is five o'clock, a dry morning, overcast to clear by eleven, a light southerly. We are just East of Plymouth, off the Modbury Road. Sir Dashford Wickham allowed us to set up camp in his park. It will require an hour to reach the Devonport ferry for Saltash.'

'Thankyou, Fisher. Eggs and toast, fifteen minutes. And don't forget yourself. I don't want to be late; all those damned Directors. Put out my better travelling suit, would you? Oh, and some hot water if you can rustle any up.'

They rolled into Plymouth and the crowds, alerted by the newspapers, roared at the odd coach, black and long, pulled by four matched blacks. Like a hearse, some said. Brunel raised the blind and waved back.

'Nothing wrong with pleasing the crowds.'

At Devonport, there was a large crowd prepared for a day out on the river. Steam ferries for Saltash departed the jetties every fifteen minutes. The Dockyard had closed for the day, offering rides in barges pulled by the Naval steam pinnaces to the hundreds of shipwrights, carpenters, leadworkers, boilermen, dollymen, finishers, rivet boys, donkey men, and drub men, as well as all the Naval seamen ashore together with their wives and families. There were fleets of private yachts and Captain's gigs and the Port Admiral's launch, all taking the tide upriver.

Aided by Naval marshals, the ferrymen kept the Devonport ferry clear and Brunel's coach rolled down the slip onboard; with a blast on the whistle, they hauled for the other shore. Brunel climbed down to gaze upriver at the bridge construction. The piers on the Western shore were all constructed, topped by the plate girder bridge. The central pier, iron clad, rose in the centre of the river like a misplaced factory chimney, a long distance from the west shore; this was the span the truss was to bridge today, his lenticular truss that he could just make out sitting on barges below the bridge. Four hundred and fifty-five feet long; never had he constructed a span of that length before but the figures added up. Hadn't he constructed the widest and flattest brick arches for the Great Western at Maidenhead and had they not settled the anticipated three inches and no more? He climbed up again and his coachman prepared to lead the horses off the ferry.

There was mayhem at Saltash. As well as the crowds landing from Plymouth, Devonport and all the smaller and more distant places like Cawsand and St. Germains, people were walking in from the Cornish side. The inns and tea-houses were overflowing, queues lining the pavement. Many private houses had opened their doors, offering a humble fare, taking advantage of the flood of visitors. His coach made for the builders' compound upriver of the town, the coachman struggling to keep the horses under control. As he arrived, there was a roar; he was recognised, the funny short man in the newspapers; they knew of his famous works that had improved the travel to London for those who could afford it. The fences were manned with police to keep out the crowds.

He went to the work sheds looking for Charles Mare, the ship builder from Blackwall who he had persuaded to build the trusses. He was with the builders, working on plans and schedules. They shook hands, Mare a hesitant smile that didn't reach his eyes.

'Well met Charles. How are you? Is all ready? Is the work in hand?'

There were a few questions from the riggers and fixers. Bolts were examined, drawings checked. There was a knock on the door.

A small crowd of fishermen stood there. At their head was a burly man, a head taller than Brunel, grey whiskers and beard, sharp eyes.

'Sir, these men are concerned at the height above the channel; they fear that their topsails will foul the bridge. I have assured them that the Admiralty has approved the height and that none of their masts will come near. Could you have a word with them?'

The fishermen were silent, awed to be addressed by the great man himself. Brunel explained the height to be left clear above high tide, spoke with knowledge of the height of their masts, reassured them that there could be no problem. He explained how the single pier had been adopted to simplify construction and to leave the tideway clear for river traffic. He spoke to them of the needs of shipping, the effect that the bridge pier would have upon the riverbed, and the minor disruption to the fish population. The fishermen were impressed and easily satisfied, as though they only needed a word from him. They asked no questions but thanked him for time, turned as a group and were escorted out of the compound.

With Mare beside him, he walked to the bridge. The land fell away and the bridge on its landed piers seemed to float through air, terminating with a few timbers before a hundred feet fall. Railings had been erected, boarding laid down, and there were tables laden with food and drink. Celebrations were already underway, ladies sitting beneath temporary shelters, men in tall top hats busy with introductions, contracts, exchanges of views and business.

Mare turned to Brunel; he appeared uneasy.

'I know you would rather be at work, sir. But the Directors insist. It is an important day for them. There are also local dignitaries. May I introduce the Mayor? They have been very helpful, with the police and other arrangements.'

"Isambard Kingdom Brunel, sir, I have the honour to welcome you to our humble town of Saltash. We are very proud that this noble edifice should erupt … no, I meant to say…"

At this point, Charles Mare took Brunel's elbow and introduced him to a line of dignitaries, from local parishes, the Dockyard, Plymouth, and the newspapers. The Directors of the Cornwall Railway and the Great Western railway watched and waited. It was their plan that was reaching fruition; they were keen to extend the line from London to the Southwest, with the expectation that passengers might take ship at Falmouth for America. They wanted everything to go well, wanted the support of the local people and the best publicity. Brunel knew most of them; he had presented his plans to them in London a year or two before and remembered resistance from some who were appalled at the radical design. We don't want some odd ship, they said. What is it? asked others. A banana boat? He had encountered such problems before. The chairman had vision, had navigated the project through the storms but needed to be re-assured; this day was important.

'Well, Brunel, this is a great day,' said one of the Directors. 'I believe you have some surprise for us and we always enjoy your surprises.'

Brunel stood before them, the wind lifting his cloak, a glass in his hand.

'Gentlemen, I give you the Tamar crossing. May it give you the joy of travel to the far West; and beyond.'

The Directors applauded, a low rumble of approval. The proof of the pudding was in the eating.

Brunel walked to the end of the bridge construction and down onto a platform that had been suspended against the end pier over the river. He stood with Charles Mare, a semaphore man, and a runner. Below him, the barges were in position, lashed to the piers and anchors set into the riverbed, the giant truss looking like some beached whale. He looked down the funnels of the giant winches on the shore, stokers moving around them. The clouds were clearing and he became aware of the vast crowd behind him and on the far shore, singing and cheering. Glancing down, he noticed a dinghy; three small boys appeared to be climbing onto the barge. They were chased away by men; Brunel wished that he were down there to welcome them and show them the wonders of bridge building. He spoke to Mare. A steam whistle sounded.

The crowds were silent. At a word from Mare and a sign from the semaphore man, the steam winches at the foot of the pier started to lift the truss. The wind had risen a little, and the truss swung, twisting out of line. Charles Mare gave a few instructions to the runner. The lines attached to the truss were adjusted and the truss swung into position. The hoisting continued.

'It's going well, Mare. Call me if you need me.'

Brunel climbed up to the bridge deck and went to speak with the Railway Directors. He wanted to allay any fears that they might have and keep his ears open for further work; he always needed more work. There was a roar from the crowds as they saw him again before they resumed their party. At least two bands were playing, large decorative banners marking their allegiance; the Devonport band was a little louder than the Saltash town band that was at least playing in tune. Hawkers moved through the crowd, loaded with food, ribbons, toys and other trinkets; a stench of cooked food hung in the air. A shriek, and he saw a girl slap a sailor across the cheek; within moments, the crowd had closed about them and nothing more could be seen.

Returning to his post, he found Mare troubled, poring over his calculations.

'I don't understand it; I have checked and rechecked, but it looks as if the truss will be four inches too short.'

Brunel smiled; he could understand how the miscalculation had been made, how the expansion joint would be fitted later, and reassured Mare. After a while, Mare smiled and apologized. Brunel felt happy, always happier when with the men, rather than the Directors. The wind blew his frockcoat up, threatened his top hat, and the steam and smoke from the winches whirled around him. The truss continued to rise, a slow inevitable progress, approaching the fixing plates.

The tide rose slowly over the mud flats and still boats arrived at the town piers, way below him; naval pinnaces prevented them from approaching the bridge. From time to time, he ascended to the bridge deck, where company and food was pressed on him; Mare never took a moment's rest. The truss was located in position by gangs working at both ends.

At one point, there was a tussle at the gates to the builders' enclosure. A band of Cornishmen, beneath a large banner declaring 'the Kingdom of Cornwall', were objecting to the bridge in principle; it was a threat to their insularity and their sovereignty. They chanted the Cornish anthem in their tongue, standing shoulder to shoulder. The police were laughing; they were mostly from Devon and they gave short thrift to these rural Cornishmen.

At three o'clock, there was a long blast from the steam whistle, declaring that the hoisting was complete. The crowd roared happily, a heady breath of alcohol and fried food. The dignitaries and guests applauded with gusto and began to leave, drifting back to the town among the crowds for further celebrations. On the bridge, fixers appeared with tools and harnesses and started the work of bolting the truss in place. Brunel watched the men work; his eyes followed the barges and other boats returning downriver, and gazed out to sea, lost in thought. An iron ship … perhaps …

He turned back to the bridge. 'A good day, Charles.' he said. Charles Mare shook his hand; he looked exhausted, relieved. Brunel alighted his coach and rolled down to Saltash where he was feted, feasted and exhausted by prodigious amounts of drink, food, toasts and speeches. Later on, he climbed into his coach and removing his hat, coat and boots, fell into a deep sleep while the coach gently went away to some quiet field.

We were up early. It's been a long night but a good'un. Dad said that we 'ad to be upriver 'fore seven or we would never make the moorings. So we were out beyond the Mole fishing off the Point, a good catch. And then I got a bit of a kip coming in; there weren't nothing to do with that southerly pushin' us home and the catch to drop at the Hoe or maybe Devonport. Dad would see to that.

Now we come up river and I'm doing the usual, scrubbin' down the decks, sluicin' out the fish safes, coiling down the ropes, while he just stands there, smokin' that stinky old pipe of his. I can see the waders on the mud flats; know the names of all of 'em. Don't need school for that; can do all the sums I need, know the names of everthin'. Mother don't know, do she? What do I want schoolin' for? Dad says I'm the best hand he's ever had (an' the cheapest).

Bridge looks huge; how they goin' to get from that side to t' other? That chimney in the middle don't look too good; too skinny. And there's a whole fleet of boats goin' up river: barges, pinnaces, tugs, the Admiral's launch, yachts, rowboats, galleys, dinghies. You wouldn't believe it! Dad had to have words with some of them, getting' in the way of us workin' boats. Think they own the river! Huh!

We tie up and Dad rows us back home to Saltash. Gosh, there are crowds everywhere. Never seen so many people in my life. Mother's in a bit of a tiz; breakfast isn't ready, the babe's squalling, and she has some tale about how some man was knocking on the door askin' for water. Well … she wouldn't turn 'im away, would she? And then there were more, offerin' money for our breakfast. What do you think of that?

I'm not missin' out on this; bugger school. So I take Jimmy with me. He's ten, quite useful if he'd just shut up. We took Dad's boat; well, he's not goin' to use it today. When he's eaten and kipped, and taken Mother upstairs for a bit, he's not goin' to be in a hurry to go out until later; maybe catch the last of the tide down and go for mackerel off the Point. They're runnin' now.

On the water, we can see everthin. There's this raft of four barges, big 'uns, reckon they borrowed 'em from Devonport. We seen the yard across river where they make these truss things, they're huge, and this raft has got this funny shape bit of iron on it, like a hull upside down; never seen anything like it. Funny sort of bridge, you'd be goin' up and down. Anyways, this thing is between the chimney and the pier our side of the river. We're Cornish, you see, not like them soft Devon boys. We pick up Jem on the way.

We drop down quiet like against one of the barges; we seen them Naval pinnaces keeping people away but they're just tourists, don't belong like us. And there's nothing upriver side. But all hell lets loose; I've only just got the painter round a bollard and this big man comes over, swearin' like a trooper and grabbin' at us. I left Jimmy and Jem to themselves; they can manage. Jem's straight off into the river; could always swim like a fish and he's away. Jimmy got caught; sorry about that but I don't see any point us both being caught. He can talk his way out of most things. So I slide under this iron truss thing and hide up in the bilge of the barge; pretty mucky ol' barge. Reckon they don't clean out their bilges too often. Dad'd have a fit if I left our bilges like this.

And then I must 'ave slept 'cause I didn't see the truss goin' up. But there it was, 'bout half way up the pier, lookin' huge. I could see a man with semaphore flags, goin' like crazy, and next to him were these two

34

men in stovepipe hats, one's smoking this cigar, could have sworn he looked at me and winked. 'Course I'm way down below him; maybe he didn't see me. I must have slept agin 'cause next thing I know we're under way and I can see the bridge clear now with that iron truss thing on top of the chimney and fixed to the pier our side.

Can't tell you much more 'bout the Bridge what I saw. Took me rest of the day to get home, on a tug in the end. But Mother, after she'd batted me over the head 'bout Jimmy, who stood there grinnin' his head off (I'll deal with 'im later), told me 'bout the bands and the crowds and the sailors in the town, all drunk, and the officials all dressed up and said that I would never see another day like that in all my life and what an idjit I was to have missed it. But my day wasn't so bad.

Gospel Pass

You can stay in the shelter of the pretty town; there are pubs, bookshops and tearooms to protect, entertain and keep you. But if you must escape the town and its delights and seek a lonely place, take the road that rises directly up the hill to the South, bending between high banks with trees arching overhead and continue, no great distance, until turning up a final slope and twisting by the banks of a rushing brook, you emerge onto a plain, on one side looking over the valley and on the other rising abruptly with a high scarp where buzzards circle lazily on rising draughts. But you haven't gone far enough; this is still the haunt of ice-cream vans and those who sit in their cars gazing at the view, windows tightly closed. You must go further where the road is squeezed against the mountain flank, the tarmac occasionally falling off to the slopes below, and rise up to the pass suspended between two dominating and imperious slopes. The road only just survives; sunk between banks, it staggers, totters on the summit, and then rushes away down the mountain valley, down to sheep farms, wind-swept woods, and a long-deserted priory. But stay; the pass is the lonely place.

Ice formed it, gouging its inexorable way South. Now the wind follows, coursing the hillside and funnelling down the road. The smooth slopes descend to the pass on either side, squeezing the road to insignificance. You seek shelter? There is none.

Everywhere is washed by wind and rain, cleaning, cutting, carrying the very ground away. Gulches break the banks, casting gravel upon the road and cutting miniature canyons. Take one of these, and seek solitude on the great slopes above where you might wander along tracks left by wild ponies or sheep. Or stumble without direction across the steep vastness, through wide gullies of acid sand where the weather has stripped the peat away. There is no path; up or down, or to either side; the terrain changes little; no plant raises its head above the cropped grass and heather. Even the thorn has transmuted into tiny bushes, leaf and bud turned in from the predatory sheep, wind and frost.

The only way to go is up, to climb this mountain to the wilderness above. So you must toil and drag yourself up, over the brow and cast yourself down, exhausted and utterly insignificant beneath the heavens, abraded and pared away by wind and rain to a vital kernel .

Neolithic Revolution

I say, old chap, things are getting rather bloody here. I thought I had created heaven on earth, everything tickety-boo. But there's trouble in heaven.

I don't know where to start. It is a while since we last communicated and then you were going on about the war between Germany and France and something with wheels (what are wheels, for goodness sake?) that goes along by itself. Well, if you will get distracted by such fantasies … I don't know how long I have to live. The young men; they are spying on me. I have so much to tell you, about war, women, and villages. Time was when old people were venerated, had all the wisdom, and were looked after; I believe you call it the Palaeolithic Period, a time of hunter-gatherers who were constantly on the move (how tiring!) and scarcely ever in touch with other tribes. But they weren't even homo sapiens sapiens, that you and I are; you know, higher beings. Or so we thought.

We have done well, very well. We gave up that feckless life of wandering and settled in villages, built houses, kept out the wild beasts, made pottery, created art, grew crops such as wheat and spelt, and kept animals; all of this I have told you before. You call it the Neolithic Revolution. But there are new developments: We explore the gene pool, eliminating the weaker strains, concentrating on a high yield. Goes for us too; our health is so good so that we are living and breeding longer; I have four women, you know, all quite strong and devoted to me, or so I thought, and quite a few children. I'm not sure how many; everybody here is related, a cousin or something. Plenty of labour available. We have been reaping good harvests, more than we need for day-to-day needs so that we can store against the winters; they are pretty vile here. I don't know how you keep warm; probably going to tell me that the house is warm all the time and all you do is stuff a bit of wood in a hole. Don't make me laugh! Anyway, we built two fine round towers to store grain to keep up with our storage needs and put up a fence, well, more a ditch and palisade, round the village to keep wild animals out.

Sounds good, doesn't it? Trouble is that some people want something for nothing and suggested that we were showing off our wealth, and getting lazy hiding behind our fence. Last Sunday Market, we were getting these off-hand looks and remarks, something about being hoity-toity. Of course, that set off our young men. They're all proud of their courage and hunting skills and their blood ran hot when they heard these insults against us. And that must have started it. One evening, when I had just settled the children and was placating a couple of my women in the usual way, there was a hooting and howling around the fence and before we had got moving, the gate was broken in and we found a few Others trying to get into our grain store; they had already taken a few goats. They didn't appreciate that our grain stores don't have doors but a special way in. And by the time they had discovered their mistake, our young men had killed a few of them and demanded that they sacrifice the rest. Said that they had taken our goats. Stolen.

You should appreciate that 'steal' is a new concept; I know there is a little 'borrowing' in the village. You expect that in a family and we're all related, somehow. So when one of my women complains that her seashell brooch has gone missing, I just tell her that it is Art for All. And we can pick one up at the next Sunday Market. But we don't expect villages to be attacking villages; there's enough land for our needs, even if you do have to chop down woods to create pasture, and we can all make a good life. Young men! I didn't know what to do; they were getting too big for their boots, challenging me, not paying the respect due to a chief. I ordered them to release the Others but they said we ought to raid the other village and get some slaves. What's a slave? They said someone to keep your bed warm, do the cooking and do the hard work. And when they weren't doing all that, look after the fields. Well, I asked, what are you going to do all day? They laughed in my face and said they could go hunting or have fun with their slaves. But I said that in that case the other villages would get strong or even band together and come and kill us all and eat our food. They went a bit quiet and then one, a nephew I think but I get a bit confused about all the relations, said that was a very good idea; they should subjugate the neighbouring village, teach them to grow our crops and join us as a Protectorate. Then we would be stronger and have more crops and animals. Where do the young get all these ideas and long words? Perhaps they are right, my time is past. But you can see where it's all going, can't you? No more peace, no more heaven.

Last night, in the Hall when we were eating and we had dealt with the usual complaints about the lack of meat, and me telling them that eating meat is not good for you if you are not brick-building all day and anyway vegetables are good for you, and when some of them had too much mead and started getting out of hand, I noticed one of my women giving the eye to that nephew. Actually, she was doing more than that; she was rolling her eyes (could have sworn that she had been painting them; what on earth for?) and opening her thighs for him to get a good look under her skins. I should have dealt with it then but another of my women was abrading me for not lying with her enough and I didn't want to admit that I could do with a rest now and then. And then this morning I found him in her straw on top of her, going like a wild hog; for a moment I admired his energy and was envious of his youth and style. But then I wanted to stick one of my sharpest stone daggers between his shoulder blades and gouge out his heart or maybe thrust it between his buttocks. But I can't bear a fight first thing in the morning; when they were done, I banished her, drove her outside the village, said she could find another place to live if she survived the wild animals. Maybe she would become a slave. I hoped it was an example to the other women. And do you know? Only an hour later, she was back in the kitchen making bread and my senior woman was calling me a pig and a beast; if I didn't get my priorities right, feminism would take over the village and the men could either get out or become slaves. It took a lot of time and effort, particularly in bed, to calm her down; she's very demanding, that one. I blame it on the Revolution or whatever you call it; men never had the time or effort for all this nonsense when they had to struggle to survive. And they call it Civilization. The nephew? Well, you can't leave things like that, can you? I garrotted him when he staggered off her and had the young men fling his body upon the hill in the sacred place for the birds to strip the bones. I haven't decided whether he will get a family funeral, a kistvaen to himself.

I thought we had better talk it all out and called a

meeting, sitting round the fire; for once, the young men seemed keen to talk things out and not challenge me. I pointed out that times were changing; with my age and experience, I pointed out how, when I was young, we didn't have the high yield wheat grains and we had to work much harder to get food and build our houses. They started yawning and making signs among themselves so I growled a bit and moved on to the matter of our safety. I said we didn't need slaves or to steal women or food; we were managing well. And we certainly did not need other villages coming and stealing and destroying our crops, our pigs and cattle; we would starve. What we needed to do was establish a Cold War, imagine an Iron Curtain (whatever that is) between them and us and stay this side. Just then, there was a rustling outside the door; one of the cousins (or nephews) leapt up and grabbed an arm that had been holding the door open. And pulled into the room a very pretty girl. She wasn't from our village; that was clear. I think you would call her a spy. The young men were inclined to lose their heads, mount her immediately and share her among themselves, but I pointed out that she was more valuable as a hostage (where did I learn these things?) and should be kept apart. But not returned to her village because she would tell them what we had been discussing. It was pretty obvious why they sent a woman; a young man would have been killed on the spot and his heart sent back. There was a lot of discussion about the Cold War; all the older men were for it but the younger men wanted to see blood flow. They didn't like the spying and the attack on our village. They liked that nephew's idea, the one whose body was lying outside on the hill. I didn't like it one bit.

But we still went to war; all the young men went, leaving the old men to do the work in the village. There was much weeping and tearing of skins from the women; I got into trouble for allowing the war and all my women refused to lie with me until the young men came back. I had the fences strengthened but that was not enough. One day, when our men were away fighting, the Others, who you call enemies, brought fire and managed to force an opening and took two of our young girls; pity they didn't take my senior woman. We hollered at them and waved our axes but they didn't take any notice. And they drove away our cattle; we would have lost them but our men, returning from a raid on their village, met them and fought. I went out with some of the older men to bring back the cattle and rescue the girls; we got the cattle but the Others had raped and slit the throats of the girls before we could get them. Our boys were stronger and killed three with arrows and captured two, who we will sacrifice in our village. Some died, theirs and ours. The women were wild when we got back, tearing their skins and hair over the dead boys and the girls and giving us older ones hell. They said that they would have talked to the other village and sorted it out; there wouldn't have been a war. Women! What do they know?

Well, the young men have won their war but they are not going to allow me to carry on as before. They won the war they say, and they are going to rule (rule?) the villages. They have subjugated the Other village (slaughtered the old people, made slaves of the young, driven off the beasts) and reinforced both villages to form a Protectorate. They will live off the wealth of both villages while the Others work for them and the young will provide protection for both villages. The Other young men will fight with them, I suppose. Now they must expect trouble from other villages; they have made themselves too important. Our women can't decide what to do or say; that's unusual. They like having slaves to do their work and, with more to trade, they will be able to buy more rings and brooches and such like. The old women are keeping quiet; they don't want to have their throats cut one dark night and they make themselves useful. But I don't think that I have long.

One night soon, a quiet blade will pierce the wall of my house and insert itself into my ribs; I pray that it will be quick, straight to the heart. I don't want any tribunal, any public dismissal; I hope that they pay me more respect. I look back on our achievements, our pottery and skull art, our animal breeding programmes and our high yield crops and our wonderful stone tools and weapons. And I wonder; why couldn't we have been happy to live quietly, carry on improving our farming, increase our trading, enjoy our art and our company, and enjoy our women and our drink? Can you tell me the answer? No, I thought not. Things haven't changed much, have they?

Hush, I hear footsteps outside. Now shall I stand and fight or shall I just lie quietly here, stiff upper lip and all that? My time is come

A Christmas Night

T'was on a nuanced night when we talked together; the door blew open as the lightning struck. A black howling hole of night it was, shattered with lightning; a roaring roaring wind that raised the dust from the floor, blew the curtains to the ceiling and extinguished our candlelit feast.

Out of the darkness they came, rolling like tumbleweed, crashing into the table, the sofa, sending chairs flying, tumbling, cursing, swearing, and finally … still. Mother turned on the light.

They stood up, barging each other, coughing, tugging at their clothes, seven of them in all. Dressed in boots with the tops turned down, heavy jackets with wide belts, knotted scarves, and broad brimmed hats that drooped with dripping wet. Still the wind whirled around us as we stared at each other.

Came a rough high sing-song voice in the roaring wind. 'You'd best be still, or you're DEAD!'

The one who had spoken stepped forward; he had

a cutlass thrust in his belt, threatened to trip him at every step, for he was not tall. Like the others. About the same as me, four feet, give or take a few inches. Not that you are counting when faced with a gang of pirates, however small they are.

'Where's the treasure? DON'T waste my time, or I'll give you a kiss of my beauty here.' He pulled out his cutlass, wagged it in our faces. Only two foot long, but awful sharp.

Father shut the door, with a slam; a sudden silence. The pirates, as one, wheeled about and advanced on him, the cutlass to the fore.

'Do you know who I am? Do you want me to do something you'll regret? Haven't you heard of BIG BILL AND THE BOYS? We're pirates on the Main, the Spanish Main, and we live one day at a time. So be very afraid; we're horribly horrible and do horrifying things.'

At which the others stuck out their chests, smirked a horrible smirk, barged each other, rolled about and started to sing a sea shanty, arms around each other's shoulders.

'Avast there, me hearties, or I'll clip your ears and send you down the HAWSE PIPE,' Big Bill roared. They stopped, silent, looking ashamed, staring at the floor.

And then to my parents, 'Now, it's Christmas time, ain't it, and I've come for my share. Where's the loot, the goodies, the CHRISTMAS PRESENTS?' Slow and clear, an awful menace in his voice, in his face. 'I'm not asking AGAIN.'

At that moment, the letterbox clattered and in fell a sheaf of letters, and one thin parcel.

'I'll start with that one,' he said, and ripped off the paper. 'Ugh! UGH! What's THIS?' He held up a thin box, a nightdress. 'What do you think I could do with this, then? Some landlubberly concoction I dare say, when all WE do is roll into our hammocks and our bunks, and snore the night away.'

Father looked at Mother, a look of love and regret.

Bill cast it aside, where it was caught by one of his gang who examined it and clasped it to his bosom. An embarrassed look at his mates. Who guffawed, pointing, quipping about their lily-livered ships boy who fancied himself in a ladies nightdress. Why, what good would he be in a real fight, when they met Hawkins or one of the others on the Main?

Big Bill turned a frightening level of red, going on purple; steam came out of his ears and he turned on his boy with a growl; the boy ran, ducked around the room, hid behind Father. 'You WAIT, young Sam, you wait until you're back on board. We'll keelhaul you, we'll hoist you at the main yard, we'll strip the skin off you and feed you to the sharks … what else do I usually threaten you lot with?' He scratched his head, and looked just like Father when he was confused and didn't know what to do. 'Now, where was I? We'll not catch the tide like this, and go down to the high seas where the waves lift us to the heavens and fish come flying aboard and easy pickings are there for all. Mate, do you have the ship ready to sail? You, HAND over the treasure, or you'll be greeting St. Peter before you greet the Baby Jesus.'

There was a silence, broken only by a slushing munching noise; the pirates had found our beef pudding and apple pie, mustard and custard, and were scooping it up in their fingers. Now and then, there was a tussle as they fought over a prize morsel, a large bit of beef or a golden piece of pie crust.

I looked at Father, and Father looked at Mother, and Mother looked at Big Bill and it didn't look as if she was going to give him any presents. She looked as if she was going to give him a good beating and I didn't fancy his chances. Big Bill swore an awful oath and grabbed me round the waist.

'Do I have me an extra ships boy?' he said with a leer. 'What do you say, lad, do you fancy a life on the high seas?'

I smiled. Shrugged. Anything seemed better than Latin Prep. Father looked at Mother. She scowled, a look that usually meant trouble for anyone, but often me.

There was a flash of lightning which lit up the room, caught us like bleached statues staring; the lights went out, and a peal of thunder cracked the sky, growing into a loud deafening rumble that went on and on, on and on, shaking the walls, the roof, the floor.

Silence. We waited.

In the darkness, there was a curious sound, half sobbing, half moaning. Big Bill had released his hold on me and I moved towards where Mother was. The lights flickered and came on.

In the middle of the floor was a mound of pirate; they had huddled together like penguins, a scrummage, heads down, backs out, all shaking.

When she saw this, Mother laughed and laughed, bent over, hands to her sides, eyes streaming.

Big Bill looked up. 'What you laughing at, woman?'

Mother couldn't speak.

'Don't you know,' he said, 'that thunderstorms are the most dangerous thing a pirate ever has to face, next to his mother? Because there is nothing, nothing we can do, out on the wide open sea. And if we are struck, it's Davy Jones locker for us, ship and all.'

The other pirates were looking around, sheepish, hands around their ears, waiting for the next lightning strike.

Mother said,' You all look as if you could do with a bit of food. Oh … seems it's all gone. Well, how about a dish of cocoa and Great-Aunt's biscuits? They're last year's, but they keep very well. If you tap them to knock out the weevils,' she added with an evil smile.

The pirates sat in a circle on the floor, I among them, and drank and chewed the awful biscuits; I showed them how to dip them in the cocoa to soften them a little and they chaffed me, called me a proper ships boy, and fell to singing again.

And after that, they stood, brushing crumbs off their coats, wiping their mouths with filthy spotted handkerchiefs, and mumbled a surprising Thankyou. A number glanced around and stuffed an extra biscuit into their pockets. They asked me again, wouldn't I like to join them?

Big Bill gave my Mother a deep bow, hat off, curling his moustaches. 'We'll bid you a grand Adieu, my Lady, and thankyou for your generous hospitality. Until we come ashore again …'

And they trooped out of the door, captain at the fore, ships boy bringing up the rear. He gave one look over his shoulder at the warmth, the table, Mother and all, and turned away with a shrug. The door closed.

Flyboy

That's it. Level out over the beach. Bank a little to starboard. Gentle breeze coming up river. Bright morning sunshine. Feet in running mode.

Much better to land on the beach; it's soft and reasonably dry. Poor Mary; she can't land on land yet. She always has to land in water where there's more room for mistakes. Trouble is, she always arrives soaked unless she's wearing that ridiculous wet-suit, the one with the slots for her wings.

So I was coming in on dry land. A good flare-out and I touched down, a gentle trot, dignified I hope. Except that I put a foot into a sand castle and went flying, ending up with my head in a young mother's lap, my mouth full of sand.

'Oh no, not one of those ridiculous flyboys!' she said. 'Why can't you keep to yourselves? You lot are weird. Get out of here; you'll frighten my daughter.'

I dragged myself up, slipping a jacket over my wings, spitting out sand, and wondering whether to make a witty response. But what was the point?

It has been the same ever since we appeared. It's difficult to say when that was because at first we were hidden away like old-fashioned crazies, out of sight out of mind. When it seemed that there quite a few of us, a special school was established but they soon discovered that we were just like other children except more creative, more likely to think of the unusual thing to do and come up with different ideas. So they closed the school and put us back into the community; a saving the government said. Back at home, we went to the local schools and did rather well in some cases. I understand that there's a Flyer at university now and do you know what he is studying? Aeronautics. What a laugh!

School was not always easy. You know how school children can be? Some of our kind were reduced to running away; I was lucky. I grew up with some good friends and they protected me from the bullies. And when they found that I could be useful, things got much easier.

Parents never learn how to deal with the appearance of wings. Tough on them though. It's not as if it's predictable; you might be one of three children with normal parents and not a Flyer among them. They don't know how we appear. When we are born, there's no sign, none at all. Just like another baby. It's a shock to the mothers though, because at about two, when the legs start working, the wings grow out of the back, small at first but sprouting fast a bit like webbed feet.

They can be uncomfortable. I could never decide how to sleep when I was a teenager and if you are a bit hot you can get a sore back. It takes years to really fly; the young ones flap their wings and make bird-like sounds. They think it helps. I suppose they think they are kinds of birds. But they're not. They are human. Just developed a bit differently. Something I learnt at school; we are all descended from birds.

At the end of the beach, I looked out over the water. There were a few girls swimming, one really attractive. It was no good. Girls usually don't like us, find us odd, sometimes are a bit frightening. We think we are just the same as other boys, apart from the wings but they don't get it. I wandered down to the ferry. A girl caught my eye and smiled. I smiled back but didn't bother to say anything.

'Cat gotcha tongue? My friend and I are just going across to the pub in the town. Wanna join us?'

'Yeah. Alright. I'm Will.'

'And I'm Janice and this is Paula.' She pointed to a fat girl who was wrestling with a back-pack, trying to sling it over her shoulders. I lifted it for her and she gave me a grateful grin.

'Where are you staying?'

'Oh, we're not on holiday. I mean, we live here. Just over the river. My mum runs a b&b place for the holiday-makers. She's really busy right now, full up with families. Where do you live?'

'Over the other side of the county. A small place; you won't have heard of it.'

The launch ground against the jetty and we climbed on. Janice pushed between Paula and me, giving her a look. It was summer, a busy time here. The ferry was full, mothers with their kids, spades and buckets. The moorings were full, and there was race going on, sailing dinghies threading their way through the moorings. Up the river, a cruise-ship was manoeuvring, turning in the crowded anchorage. Down river, a string of yachts was coming up. A strong ebb was running.

The ferry pulled away, chugging upstream. The ferryman was short-handed and asked some lad to take the tiller while he went around collecting money. The cruise-ship had completed its turn and was coming towards us, gathering speed. It hooted loudly, four long blasts. The lad at the tiller laughed.

'Who do they think they are?'

Downstream, the yachts had struck a band of sheltered water and had come on fast, almost up to us. They had spread out, the larger boats ploughing past the small ones, pushing the ship over towards us.

It seemed to take everyone by surprise. The ferryman looked up, swore and rushed for the tiller. At that moment, the lad bent down to look at his mobile phone and the launch swerved towards the ship, sending the ferryman sprawling on the floor among bags and feet. The ship, turning ponderously like a huge truck, hit the launch, swinging us round and dragging us along as the launch began to fill.

Janice looked scared, terrified. Paula dived into the river but Janice froze, the water rising around her legs. I stripped off my jacket and spread my wings; she stared, but didn't struggle as I rose above the water with her in my arms.

We are not very strong as flyers. We get teased, told to go fly the Channel with a suitcase in our arms. But we can't do it; we can only fly a few miles and we can't lift heavy weights, at least not for any distance. They say that with a little practice, we could fly much further but it would take an awful lot of energy. I can't see myself doing it.

I lifted her over the water, and was between the moored yachts when I felt a buffet and was spun round, dropping Janice into the water. I looked round and saw a Flyer in black, laughing at me and flying faster than any Flyer that I knew. I fell onto the beach. Paula was doing well with Janice struggling behind her and I flew back to the launch; the ship had stopped and a fleet of small boats surrounded the launch so I flew back to Janice. She was wading out of the water.

'So you're one of those, you bastard. Dropped me in the drink.'

'I was trying to help you. But... didn't you see it?'

'What are you talking about? You just dropped me in the drink. Look, everything's soaked. Why don't you bugger off? Me and Paula will look after ourselves. Bloody Flyboys.'

And they turned their backs and walked up the beach. I scanned the sky, looking for the black Flyer; who was he, where had he come from? All the Flyers I knew were friendly; this black one was something new. We hung together, us Flyers; sometimes I felt that there was some telepathy between us. We could feel if one of us was near, recognise signals of pleasure or distress. Quite often, if you were in trouble, a Flyer would appear, to help or perhaps simply to give support. We shared problems and felt special. But the black Flyer had broken all the rules; was he a new breed, a variant, or simply one that had gone wrong?

I boarded the other ferry; Janice and Paula ignored me, at least Janice did. Paula was trying to catch my eye but I wasn't in the mood.

The town was crowded. Visitors filled the streets, pouring in and out of the shops, hanging out of the pubs, lined up on the quay staring at the yachts. I joined them, wandering down the road, stopping to buy a pasty and settling on a spare place at a bench looking out over the water. It was hot and I felt uncomfortable, my wings drying slowly in my jacket. Wouldn't it be nice to strip off and spread them out to dry like a cormorant? I could imagine the hostility of the people around me. There would be a small riot, women hustling their children away from 'the monster' and men protecting them, pushing me away. There would be the usual names: 'freak', 'bloody flyboys', 'human bat', and the rest. It was such a pity; we could be useful to the emergency services, faster and lighter than firemen in rescuing people off roofs, we could rescue from water and fly help into difficult locations. But all we got was abuse as though we should be performing miracles, Superman or Batman, not helping and on a lesser scale. I sighed. A man looked at me.

'Beautiful place, isn'it? Reckon it would be lovely to live here. You live here?'

'No ... no, I'm just visiting,' I said.

'Yeah. I come down from Bristol, yesterday. Terrible roads an' all but we got the 'van here, lovely site, terrific views. I'd come down here every holiday 'cept my missus loves Spain. You know, beach and sun. Hate it myself, getting all hot and burnt up. Takes all sorts. Where are you staying?'

'Oh, I'm only here for the day.'

'What? You local, or something? ... Here, what's that? Looks like a fire, that big house on the hill there.'

'Where? Oh no.'

'There's a kid on the roof; can you see? Hope the fire-engine doesn't take too long. Gawd help her!'

I slipped away; now I could prove something. "Flyboy saves life". That would help us, move things along. I hurried up an alley, heading for the house. At the top, some-one was leaning against the wall, chatting into a 'phone or something. As I hurried past, a foot shot out, and I sprawled across the pavement into the road, just avoiding a car coming along. I rolled into the gutter, craning to see who had tripped me. But there was nobody there. I stumbled to my feet; my elbows were sore, and my legs bleeding, but my wings felt all right. I limped up the hill as a fire engine went past, klaxon blaring.

At the house, it was so hot you couldn't get near; the firemen were spraying water, but it was too dangerous to put a ladder up to the roof. They said. That kid was hanging on, the other end from the flames; what was wrong with the firemen? I'd had enough; I stripped down and spread my wings. But … arms grabbed me from behind.

' So, you're going to cause trouble, are you? Think you can show off while we have a real emergency?'

I squinted round; a fireman was grasping my arms, breathing hard. He looked awfully hot in his uniform. Behind him, I saw a figure in black running away. I tried to pull away, and his helmet fell off; he dropped an arm to reach it, and I slipped away, running around the house, and taking off to soar over the roof.

The kid, a small girl, looked at me in horror, and started to scream 'Mummy, Mummy, there's a monster up here!'

'Come on, I'll save you.'

'No, no, I can't … you're –'

At that moment, a section of roof collapsed beside her, with flames roaring up, a hot blast of air. As she looked away, I gathered her up in my arms and lifted off the roof. My wings were singeing and I was trying, flapping as hard as I could as I dropped down towards the garden, a crowd of people, firemen and parents, hot, panting … I knew no more.

A cool breeze washed over me. I turned and my wings stabbed with pain; I rolled onto my front. The grass beneath me was neatly clipped and a worm slipped away from my hand. A smart ladies shoe stopped in front of my nose.

'Are you … I mean … it was very good of you. Will you be all right?'

I sat up, gripping my arms around me. It had become cool, clouds over the sun, a fresh onshore breeze. The flames had disappeared, and the firemen were rolling up the hoses.

'Where is she? Is she all right?'

'Yes, I think so. Her mother took her to the hospital; they haven't come back yet.'

'How long have I … Oh, never mind.' I hauled myself to my feet, and set off down the road.

Bacon Roll

It was a good morning. Low cloud hung over the roofs and distant hills, but it wasn't raining; I wouldn't need a mac. My wife, or She-who-must-be-obeyed (after she had seen it on the telly, she reminded me often enough), hadn't insisted I wear a scarf or hat. She had been so busy talking to her sister, who we don't often see, that she barely said 'goodbye' as I went out the door.

They had told me where the station was, and when to get off. I felt quite sprightly, quite young; I was looking forward time on my own. Since I'd retired, the wife was always around. We'd been cooped up in the car all the way from Coventry, shut in by lorries and cars hogging the outside lane. I like driving but I don't like traffic. Give me a clear road across the moors, with grass down the middle.

They told me that the city wasn't like Coventry, a bit bigger and rougher. But I wanted to get downtown; I wanted to find a decent café and have a bacon roll. If my brother-in-law had been alive, we would have had a proper breakfast, not some little bowl of muesli and a cup of tea. It doesn't keep a man going until elevenses.

I got to the station; there's no ticket office, or Station Master, but there are notices. I had to put my glasses on to read them and a young woman came and helped me. You put coins in the machine and the ticket comes out; it will even give change if you need it. But the machine must have run out of change and I didn't want to make a fuss in front of the nice woman so I left it, although she did tut-tut for me. I looked at the timetable and there was a train in three minutes. Three minutes! At home, we get used to waiting thirty, more sometimes! And that's just for a bus.

It arrived, not noisy and fast like the main line trains, but slid in and the doors slid open. No button pushing, no scramble for seats, no big step up. Marvellous! I stepped in, and turned to the nice young woman.

'You've got a lovely shuttle.'

But she had just gone and sat down; perhaps she didn't hear me. Before I could choose a seat, the doors closed and the train started. My legs aren't what they used to be; I sat down quickly by the window on the other side so I could look at the view. There wasn't much to look at; it must be an old line, because the fencing and track all looked a bit battered. The buildings were mostly Victorian, terrace houses and shops and then warehouses where they'd been pulled down. I didn't

63

see any countryside which was a pity. The train wasn't crowded; a few little children and middle-aged people like myself going shopping. Just chatting, no radios or telephones.

After a while, we came into another station; I think it was the third one but I can't be sure. It was larger, all concrete with a bridge over the track and an office and a signal box. There was a crowd on the other platform, with mothers holding little children back from the edge. A train came in going the other way and stopped. You could see right through to the other platform, people getting off and on and sitting down. And then, almost opposite me in the other train, I noticed this boy sitting by the window. At first, I didn't want to look at him. I'm not one for staring, not like my wife; she's terrible. But I realised that he was smoking with a No Smoking sign right over his head; and he was slouching in his seat, feet up on the opposite bench.

I don't like trouble. I've never had a fight, just a few nasty experiences like everyone else. But this wasn't like being in the open where he could get rough with me. Although we were only five feet apart, there were two windows between us and my train was about to leave. Someone ought to tell him how unsociable he was being; so I said,

'You little bugger! What do you think you're doing? Get your filthy feet off of that seat, and get rid of that fag!'

I was saying it to myself but I noticed the woman

across from my seat giving me a funny look. The boy saw me and got up, shaking his fist at me with a really ugly look. I wasn't having any of that.

'You ugly bastard,' I said, 'why don't you have some respect?'

I got that funny look from the woman opposite again and I said to her,

'Didn't you see? That young man's got no respect, he's just a vandal!'

She didn't look at me again. He glowered at me and made a rude sign, and then my train started. And as it moved, we got closer and closer until I was looking right into his eyes; it was like looking into an angry dog's eyes. And then we were past.

And that was the end of it; we were on trains going in opposite directions and I would never see him again. I'm not the sort that looks for a fight. But you get it from time to time, don't you? This fear, of being assaulted, or mugged, or robbed; it is natural to avoid violence. You keep yourself safe, rather than stand up for what you believe, even if you see someone else getting it; maybe that's what the German people felt like under the Nazis. I wondered why I had stood up to him and I realised that I'd never before had the chance to stand up for myself, to stand up for proper values. It's easy to do nothing, isn't it? For years, I'd sat at the same desk in the big Inland Revenue office while young managers, all climbing up the ladder of promotion, told me what to do without knowing the job themselves. But I couldn't do or say anything and I had my pension to consider.

I said I'd had a few nasty experiences. But generally, it's not something that happens to oneself. Only to other people. Even when it's terrible, earthquakes and floods, many people killed, one is shocked but the shock passes fast because it's hard to relate to, not real.

Then something real does happen. A few years back, I was driving home and a car pulled alongside me on the bypass, going 50 miles an hour; there was this guy waving his fist at me. I didn't know what he was on about; I'd never seen him before. He wanted me to pull in but no way was I going to pull in with a mad guy. Perhaps he was on drugs or drink; his girlfriend was driving. After a while, I couldn't see him any more and I didn't believe that he would attack me in front of other people. I had to stop at a roundabout, between a filling station and a school; children were coming out, all over the road. Suddenly a fist came through my window and he hit me in the face, almost breaking my nose. I was stunned; I'd moved on mentally, not believing that the threat was real. It was real enough; I got out and their car was just behind. I stood in front of it, pointing at the girl behind the wheel and dripping blood on the bonnet; she was shocked and he was urging her to get away. They drove off through the filling station and disappeared.

Somebody on the pavement said he'd seen everything that happened and would be a witness; he gave me a piece of paper with a phone number. I felt dizzy, had difficulty writing down the registration number, and drove to a police station; the officer was worried about me and said I ought to be in hospital and not driving. They never did catch that bloke; found out where he lived, but they never caught up with him. You can see, it makes you feel put on, suffering violence like that. And what can you do? It's not as though you could stand up to someone like that; they will always beat you, the violent ones.

This is the type of violence that you associate with streets and yobs, the most real; you never dream of having contact with hitmen or an organised crime syndicate that one reads of in the newspapers. They won't be concerned with your life; you are a not nearly rich enough to be interesting. Still, you hear tales of people disappearing and wonder.

I knew this bass player who was having an affair with the wife of a friend who was working abroad; this had been going on for some time but they were careful never to speak of it. After a gig, they would go to the nearest club, drink until three, and then return to their b and b; they always had landladies who were used to bands and their hours. One night, the bass player stumbled into the house where he was staying, couldn't find the light switch, and started up the stairs in the dark. He hadn't gone far when the landing light came on above him; he stopped, squinting up into the light. At the head of the stairs was a smartly dressed man, polished black shoes, dark trousers with a crease, a dark overcoat, shirt and tie. The man looked down at him without expression.

'Are you Mr Basham?' he asked.

The bass player nodded, pissed and confused. The man went on.

'You are never to see Mrs Smith again, you understand?'

As he said this, he opened his coat and showed him a pistol, in a holster. Then this man left, as quiet and polite as ever, and the bass player staggered up to his bed. But he never did see Mrs. Smith again. You wouldn't, would you?

Some people just love a bit of violence. There was this film called 'Fight Club', where they looked to get hurt. When I was doing my National Service in the Army, there were always blokes looking for a scrap; the officers looked the other way when there was a fight in the barracks. I don't know how they got away with it; perhaps they thought it made them tough. I remember when I went to see the wrestling; that was an ugly sight. These women were in the gallery, hanging over the rail, trying to knock the fighters out with their handbags. Talk about violence! They loved it. I suppose it gave them some sort of buzz. I've never talked to the wife about it; she's not like that.

A friend of mine played in a band, a rough sort of life in rough places. He told me of one club where the manager said, 'When I give you the signal, you go through that door and stay there until I tell you.'

It happened every night. It was a question of when the fight would break out, not if. He peeped out once and there were chairs and bottles flying everywhere. The band had to wait while the fight burned itself out and then come out and carry on playing. They never saw police or ambulance; it looked as if the local lads had to work off steam. The band never had any trouble.

After a few more stations, we went underground into a big tunnel, sometimes with sky above, and then we arrived at my station. A lot of people got off because it's the main shopping district; they were in a hurry. I got off the train in time and started up the corridor; it was big and bright, all tiled with lots of lights and decorations on the walls, posters of places to go and see. I wasn't in a hurry, enjoying the posters, so I wasn't surprised when I found myself all alone. But I'm downtown; I don't think of being afraid. Now, I want a bacon roll.

All of a sudden, this bloke came round the corner; I've seen him before and it took me a moment to remember where it was. Then my first thought was, oh no! I'm in trouble. Then I thought, perhaps he won't recognise me; why should he?

I carried on walking, as though he was a stranger. I hadn't gone more than half a dozen steps when I realised he was staring hard at me, and that he had made me; I looked behind and there was nobody there and I think I stopped walking. He raised his fist; he can't have been more than five yards away and I felt sick.

At that moment, there were two more men behind him, dressed in casual dark clothes and another one in front of him. Oh no, not a gang! I thought about running but they were much younger than me and I wouldn't get very far. I edged back against the wall.

I remember thinking that I had made a mistake and then I looked at his face and thought about the moors that we had driven over and how the wife had said, 'How do the sheep keep dry in the rain?'

And none of it made sense; the mind just switched off. Is that how it is when you know you're going to die or have a crash? Time stood still; I couldn't tell you how long.

The man who was in front of him had stopped and was talking to me; I didn't hear him at first, I couldn't understand what was going on. He was holding something in his hand but I didn't have my glasses on. And he wasn't hitting me.

After a while, I realised he was asking me something.

'I'm a police officer. Do you know this man?'

I looked past him and the two men behind him were holding the boy, one on either side, and one was getting a set of handcuffs out. The boy looked so young and not threatening, just rather lost like a whipped dog.

'No ... well, yes; I saw him on a train.'

'Where was this sir?'

'I don't know; I don't live here. But it was in the north part of your city. He was in a train going the other way, about half an hour ago.'

'So, why does he want to threaten you?'

' I … well, I saw him with his feet on the seat, smoking, and I told him off …'

'From another train?' The officer had a funny look on his face, as though he couldn't decide whether to laugh. 'Well, sir, you needn't worry about him now; we've been looking for him for a while.'

'What for, officer?'

'Oh, a number of things. You wouldn't want to know. Let's just say that it was a good thing we caught up with him at that moment.'

I said, 'Thankyou, officer.'

I don't remember anything after that, and when I woke up, I was sitting on the floor, and the officer was taking my pulse. He was worried about me, wondered if I was suffering from shock.

I said, 'Thankyou, Officer. It's been a bit of a shake-up. I think I'll just take the train back.'

I never did get that bacon roll.

The Night Before ...

The day dawns late, light creeping beneath my eyelids from a deep sky, birdless with white clouds. My nose itches; what is this? An appalling aroma pervades the room; it clings and seeps into my consciousness. I can't name this odour but it is sickeningly familiar. Memory is creeping back, splinter by splinter, as I seek to uncover the actions of the night before. My body is dead to me; my limbs recumbent like fallen masonry. Grit fills my eyes; at first, light is all I see. Let time pass, and lubricate the feeble cogs of my mind. Only to find shards of memory that threaten and stun.

No, not awake yet. My body is heavy and clumsy; instructions to roll over are blurred and protracted. Eventually raising myself to my knees, a spike pierces my head and I topple forward onto the bed, inert. More time passes, measured in breaths that earn me respite from action. Sleep, how nice it would be to sleep; but something presses me on. What is this? I am wearing a bizarre collection of pyjamas, underclothes and trousers; more confusion in the memory. I raise myself to my knees again and squinting to protect my eyes, drag myself bathroomward, legs trailing behind me, where I collapse onto the seat and let go. Hideous issue, appalling smell! I haven't dared look into the mirror; I'm afraid that I might not recognize what I see. I tear off a few clothes; it feels better. I am still stunned with partial memory, painful glimpses of a long evening.

Must have coffee, and the first of the day … my clothes stink, and I shy away from the sink cluttered with filthy crockery, taking a stained mug and pouring a strong dose of black coffee. My stomach rises up, turns on me, rebels, and a moment later I am kneeling facedown in the lavatory pan; interesting, there doesn't seem to be much to evacuate. Quite content to huddle there, hugging the bowl, waiting for … what? Hauling myself to my feet, I sink my face into the basin, turning on the cold tap to douche my pain. Return to the kitchen; a slice of stale bread thrust into the toaster, and another gulp of black coffee. This time, as my stomach prepares for mutiny, I grab an empty milk bottle, fill it at the tap and attempt to drown my stomach. It churns, producing a loud belch and an unusual noise; I stand absolutely still. Stillness is a most desirable state while I rummage around the various parts of my body and mind, analysing responses, categorising priorities and putting off action.

After a little while I'm able to open my eyes and

consume the rest of the toast. I turn to the window; to my surprise there seems to be little change. It's still morning. Time to dress; time to clothe myself in something halfway decent before I brave the world.

Whatever happened last night I shall learn the hard way of course through 'friends' and the emptiness of my wallet, though I shall have to be sure not to believe all the tales they tell me – not swimming in the river, or knocking up all the young girls or kicking over ol' man Sweedman's dustbin (well maybe that one's true, there seems to be a dent on the tip of my boot). But what happened after the first pub, when we said we should go out on the town, cast all cares to the wind, have a night to remember? Whose idea was that? Mine? In any case, what can I remember? Strange, a night to remember is usually the last thing that one can recall.

But yes, oh yes, there was that dark bar with the music, really strong, Blues with a bit of rock, and you just had to dance... The women, they were all dancing and we didn't want to be pushed aside so we were there too ... and the band, what was their name, can't remember but they were good, so strong, such guitar solos, those guitarists were great, and that big lead singer playing bass... Wish I could remember his name! We were having such a good time and then, oh gosh, oh no!

Didn't I say I could play bass really well, some stupid boast about playing blues with John Mayall and

Brian Eno and Clapton said join me! I surely didn't do that! Took his bass off him, yes oh yes that bass solo when the club went quiet. I thought my playing must be magic but maybe …and then I fell off the stage… maybe not … didn't hurt but look here there's the bruise on my backside … did I play at all? … Whose bass was it? And what happened when I fell where was the bass oh crikey was that why they moved us out the door rather sharpish not that we noticed … whose bass can't have been mine it's there in the corner. But won't go there again in a hurry, if only I knew where it was … or who was there. There was the hot-dog stand, here's the ketchup stain. Was that the end? How did I get home? Oh no, we didn't, did we? No please not her, not round at my ex! Whose idea was that! No, no, it can't have been am I sick or something the door opened and it was late and she just stood there in her night clothes not very happy to see me … did I really kneel on the step in front of her before throwing up on her nightgown … was that me? Can't have been I'm not that mad am I … no I don't want to know I can't handle that right now need another fag shit the packet's empty must get out where's the key and money can't seem to find anything better go down Dave's he'll help … shit it's bright outside … where are my shoes? Oh bugger it, forget them I'll just cruise like a hippy chick … yeah let's cruise … oh no is that the bell maybe it's Dave …

'Morning, officer … What can I do for you? Wha

… what's that you got there? … a broken bass?! Oh no, who … wha …'

Coffeebar

'Excuse me, do you mind if I take this seat?'

She looks up, taking in nothing, waves vaguely and retreats behind her laptop. The essay is trying her; it has been all morning while she consumed black coffee after black coffee, trying to eradicate a mild hangover. As she pursues the question, it seems to evade her. She wishes that the research in the library had been more thorough. Bugger. She does not notice the man who sits opposite, studying her with an innocent mixture of curiosity and frustration.

The man sits still, his coffee untouched. He is tired; feels his muscles settling in his legs, head drooping slightly, eyes heavy. He has been on the road for a long time, it seems. And the girl is a distraction, a distraction that he welcomes with an unexpected surge of interest. He looks at her; not First Year, that is certain. There is a maturity in the clothes, a wariness around the eyes. Signs of a misspent night; he wonders where she has been, with whom, how late. He watches her as she groans, fumbles in her bag and rising, goes to the counter for more coffee, leaving laptop, notes and all untended. He takes in her writing and the text books and concludes that she is studying History, or perhaps Economics. Her notes stray over the pages, sagging over the lines as though written in haste.

Three buses block the window, heavy with passengers who stare down at the coffee shop with as much interest as they would watch dogs mating. A pigeon flies down between bus and window, soaring above pedestrians' heads; one arm is raised in protest.

She returns and settles on the bench; she becomes aware that she left her bag on the seat, and feeling a little foolish, looks at the man for the first time. She wonders why he has not tasted his coffee. He is not young, certainly not a student, nor even an MA or Phd; he has a well travelled air, a weathered tan, a practical watch, a choice of clothes that is not dictated by fashion or budget. His hair is clipped short, a hint of grey. He is not looking at her; at least, she doesn't think he is but she is not sure. He seems to have an air of self confidence, of the type who can handle himself in any situation; she has known one student only like that and he was ex-Army. Something special. She wonders if he has ever killed anyone. And she wonders whether he would be a good fuck, imaginative, caring, interested in his partner as well as his own satisfaction. She moves a little in the seat, feels unaccountably warm.

He is studying her. He notes her moving on the

seat and wonders. She is not working but sipping her coffee, looking back at him every few minutes; perhaps she is unsure of herself. He looks at her bag, her clothes and her computer. It is not likely that she is a wealthy student; her things look well worn but of good quality, chosen with good taste, chosen to last. They look like the clothes that her mother might have kitted her out in before University, clothes that she has not felt necessary to discard in favour of student fashion. He wonders if the same conservative taste in clothes extends to her behaviour, whether she follows safe routines and decisions.

She stares at her screen while her mind wanders, over the essay and away, back to last night. It was a very good evening, Hall and JCR, which developed into a very good night, a new lover in a new College. Pity about the work; she had hoped for a break this term, after years of school exams (she had been such a good pupil) and a dedicated First Year. But she is growing up, leaving the earnest girl behind, blooming into a modern woman, avaricious and impatient. She forces herself back to work, forces herself to forget the pleasures of last night that had flooded into her mind. She thinks no longer of the man opposite who cannot help her with her essay and who is no more than a distraction. She sets him aside with a toss of her head.

She knows that she is skating on thin ice, the subject sliding away from her, ungraspable; with a little effort, she might have emerged from next week's tutorial with the smug satisfaction of staying ahead of the game. That's it, she thinks. It's all a game, with high stakes, played with privilege and brains: the privilege of the best University and the brains that succeeded in securing a place and holding onto it. While she plays other games, social and sexual. Not for her the dire exhaustion of the games field, or strenuous exercise on the river. She can leave that to those who have nothing better to do, to those whose priorities remain the same since school playing-fields.

He watches her work; she is a wanderer. He knows the different ways that people work, the task completer, the assiduous studier, the vague dasher, the lazy and the hopeless. She is a wanderer, fast flashes of work broken by dreaming or gazing out of the window as though thinking. But he does not believe that she is thinking about her work; he believes that her thoughts have wandered from the task in hand and she has followed them wherever they take her. Ah yes! That little smirk, was that the boy of last night, some little aberration or quirk? He is happy watching her; she is not unattractive, a certain feline sexuality mixed with the remnants of the pretty little girl that she certainly was. She turns back to work, catching his eye. She frowns, sucks a pencil, starts typing furiously. He smiles for the first time. And relaxes. It is as though he has made contact with an alien people and they are not threatening.

He thinks of the last fortnight, the long journey from out of the danger zone, a state of suspended alarm. It would be nice, he thinks, to return to a life of supposed security, if it still exists. But he has doubts that it exists anymore, anywhere.

She pauses in her typing; she wishes that her tutor did not have such high expectations of her. He expects the work to develop towards a sound First. With a career afterwards that would keep her interested and well paid and reward the country in some way; perhaps the Civil Service or a high rank in the NHS. Not an academic. She sighs briefly, gazing down at the table. And begins to wonder about the man. He is not happy; she believes she has enough experience of men to know that the man opposite is not happy. She wonders what would make him happy. With a rare flash of altruism, she thinks of ways that she might make him happy, that would bring her pleasure in the doing. Was he a poor man? She doubts it. His clothes were not cheap; outdoor clothes of recognisable brands, good shoes; she looked when she returned with the coffee. Was he an adventurer, in people? She doubts that too, does not think that he is insignificant enough to need to dominate or distract women for his own self-belief. She begins to dream of ways that they might start a conversation, ways that she might learn about him.

Sitting in the crowded coffee bar, he begins to feel lonely as he never did in the field. The girl is part of this thriving University City, along with all the other people in the bar excepting the odd tourist, easily identifiable by a combination of hesitations, ignorance of the local customs, assumed nonchalance and smart clothes. Does he look like a tourist in these new clothes that he bought in London a few days ago? What does it matter? Except that perhaps he would like to be taken as a man who always had a destination, a vital purpose that would set him apart from tourists, who, by definition, wander the highways and low ways. He feels the lack of human contact, lack of home and base. For a time, he is lost in images of the recent past, hiding out in cellars with other correspondents, a photographer shot by a sniper, had known him well, a country riven by war, no care for the ordinary people, children.

She is sure now; he is not a man to be taken lightly. He is a real man, as there are few real men in the world. He would not appreciate the games that she was accustomed to play with the boys in the Colleges, the so-called 'young gentlemen' as the porters and scouts called them. He would require serious undivided attention, a quick learning of his rules, and after that … maybe rewards beyond anything that she had experienced. She believes that he is a provider, a man who does not expect his women to pay their own way. She is not unhappy about paying her own way; indeed, she expects, when married, to have an equal and sharing existence and to work for that end. But the man opposite would not want that; he would respect her in an old-fashioned way and keep her, expecting her to be there for him as he returned from an adventure, or exploration, or a mission. Whatever he did.

He is slow, returning to the present. And briefly full of grief that a way of life has passed for him, as awful as it was, and he must adapt to a new life. Unfamiliar words have been dropped before him: job, work, pension, commuting. He does not know the world of these words, the world to which, presumably, all the citizens sitting around him, excepting the students, belong in a real way, depending upon the rules of this alien world and the rewards. He wants a different way, a way to belong still to his old world, to avoid having to adapt to their world of 'jobs' and 'hours'; he finds no pleasure in the conceiving of those. He does not think of escaping his destiny but he does think of placing himself outside of it in some genuinely fresh environment. He tastes the coffee, now cold, and returns the mug to the table.

A sudden hailstorm thrashes the window, bringing all to stare, in relief or despair. Reminded of other storms, he looks out, remembering other places, as pedestrians scurry away, huddled under hats and umbrellas, the street clearing as if under fire. Now where was it, that sudden clearing of a street? Africa, or Beirut? Cambodia, or Paris?

What if she did not complete this essay? Never completed another essay? She assumed that she would find a job but she did not relish the idea of low pay, some minimal way of paying bills and providing a little cash to escape sometimes. What would her parents say? So proud of her achievements, they had delivered her to the University each term from their Northern town without complaint. They had furnished her with an allowance to supplement her student grant and they had helped her purchase clothes, glasses, mugs and the other little necessities of an undergraduate's life. When would she be free of obligation and pay back to society what she had been told she owed? She dreams of other ways out, other ways to spend a life that would be rewarding, ways that even her parents might accept. Like marriage to a very rich man. Or research in some far foreign country.

He wonders whether the 'job' is the main thing, or just a means to an end, the end being a happy shared life where both partners contribute to their joint bliss. A life worth living for the shared pleasures and memories, diluted, perhaps thankfully, with time shared with other workers, limited hours in the day. Were not many women bound to the idea of a life like that, children and all that went with them? What about the young woman across the table? Will she end up married, putting all her learning behind her to bring up a family, provide evening meals and remember the correct programmes for the washing machine? What was this university course for?

What was all this University for? Why did she need this thinking degree simply to have a job for the rest of her life? She forgets that her degree would earn her a high paying job with many rewards and an earlier retirement. She forgets that an early exit from University would earn her a low-paying job, probably monotonous, certainly boring and menial. She dreams of a life free of essays and deadlines and of satisfying teachers; she forgets her free student life. But life in the future has little shape; for now, the sun shines, friends are always available, travel abroad occurs frequently, homes are comfortable and shopping is no problem. Best to remain a student for now? And it will end next year with a crash, a sudden descent into 'adult' life. She knows that but refuses to consider it.

He wonders whether it is possible or if it would be construed as an assault. What if he was to make a proposal to her, unbinding of course, a proposal that she leave this stressful life and travel with him? He has money, it will last a while; they could have fun, a full life not tied to duty and necessity. And when money runs short, the time will have been reached when they would have come to realise, when they would know whether they were in it for the long haul, in it for life. And then they would have to work, perhaps together.

She is tired, tired from the night before and tired of working, brain draining away on some essay that will be of no use to her after University. She wonders what it would be like to simply get up from this bench, leaving laptop, notebooks and all academia, and leave with the man. To … pass time, pass days in a man's company; running away, her parents would call it. Escaping, more like.

He gets up and leaves. A last look back, at dissipating possibilities. She is working.

She is staring at her screen but sees nothing, feeling the wrench, the swing of her world. Is it too late? Could she get up and chase him? What would he say? Who is he, after all? Would he not think her a stupid student? What is she thinking of? She returns to her essay, in a fury.

The Artist

Ben sat gasping on the bench in Upper Bond Street, next to Winston Churchill, who was stiffly bronze. His heartbeats deafened him as he struggled to regain breath. The street was empty, and he could hear nothing, apart from the distant rumble of traffic from the Strand and Oxford Street. He sat back, breathing more easily. A voice behind him spoke.

'Hiding with Churchill? I don't think he can help you!'

One sunny morning in July three months before, Ben was talking with his tutor; his head was buzzing and he felt sick. The end of year celebrations at his northern Art School had gone on too long and he had surfaced late for the appointment.

'You did very well, Ben. We would be expecting someone like you to go to the Royal College. I went to their last exhibition; there was some lad from around here called David Hockney, making quite a stir. But

I'm afraid you won't get a grant, and I guess your father can't support you … No, I thought not. Well, you could get a job down there and work while you are at the College. But there is an alternative, if you don't want any more art school.'

Ben looked up. He liked painting; it was his thing. He had tried a bit of guitar and writing songs but painting was the only thing that absorbed him.

'Is my work saleable in London?'

'Yes, I should think so. Have you been looking at the magazines? All that American stuff? Not my idea of art, but things are changing fast and if you are thinking of working there, you would have to be prepared to change to keep a gallery happy. Have a think about it, let me know. I could put you in touch with someone. I'll be around for a few days.' Sucking on his pipe, he wandered off in the direction of the First Year studios.

Ben felt dazed by the success of his end-of-year exhibition and his tutor's comments. Surely, he didn't need any more education; it was pricey and why couldn't he sell his own work and build up a reputation? At home, his father started grumbling about the need to get a job, settle down. But Ben felt modern times pulling him away from the background of his family and friends with their limited aspirations and long evenings in the pub or dancehall. He wanted something new and challenging; London was the place to go.

He borrowed a hundred pounds from his father, promising that he would come back and get a job if he made no money in six months, and took the bus to London. Armed with his tutor's reference, he presented himself at a small Cork Street gallery bearing four canvases and a small portfolio of drawings.

The director, dressed in a pinstripe suit, looked him up and down, noting the worn trousers, workman's boots and rough jacket.

'I hear great things of you,' he said. 'Have a seat.'

The portfolio was opened, the canvases spread out and the director took his time, looking at the canvases closely.

'Do you have any more of these?' he asked.

'Yes. Ten I'm happy with but … there are a few others that haven't quite got there …'

'When could you have them here?'

'I don't know but if you …'

'This style of yours is unusual; reminds me a bit of Vaughan. You know his work? Good. I think we could offer you an exhibition; would that interest you? Usual terms and if all goes well we could talk about a contract.'

'That sounds great, but … when do you want the others?'

'Can you get them to me sometime next week? And by the way, I appreciate that your garb matches your paintings but we prefer our artists to be a little more presentable. Here, let me loan you a hundred pounds; it can come out of sales. Get yourself some new clothes.'

Ben took the bus back North; he stayed one week and returned to London with all his work. The secretary at the gallery had been helpful and suggested where he might find lodgings and a studio. Before long, he was hard at work, completing pictures for his first London exhibition.

The Private View was a mixture of terror and excitement. He found himself the centre of attention, society ladies bearing down on him, praising and asking questions and bearing invitations. The wine went straight to his head and everything began to reel as he collapsed onto the sofa where a nice girl held his hand. He woke up next morning in a strange bedroom but the nice girl was brusque.

'Wake up; I have to go to work. Can you let yourself out?'

'What you doing this evening? We could go to the pictures ...'

'I'm tied up this evening, actually. Look, why don't you leave me your number?' And she was gone.

Some pictures had sold and a little money flowed into his new bank account; he had not realised the size of the gallery's cut. In the evenings, he met a group of young artists at a pub in Pimlico. A young student from Camberwell Art School took him in hand.

'Hey man, where you from? Cool! Are you alright for a studio? I could find you a nice one. You're a lucky bugger having a gallery. Most of us have to work for years before we get one. The name's Zac.'

'I don't get much money out of it. The gallery takes at least half.'

'Half? Could be worse. Why don't you take me down there one day? I'd like to see your work.'

At the gallery, Zac seemed preoccupied but asked about northern artists. The director came in and Ben introduced him. Zac brightened and started boasting of exhibitions and contacts that Ben suspected did not exist. Ben was embarrassed and wandered off but the director seemed unconcerned and chatted to Zac for some time. Eventually, the two young artists left. Ben asked him what they had been talking about.

'Oh, nothing in particular,' said Zac. 'He was just asking about old friends at Camberwell; that sort of thing.'

Ben felt a doubt growing in his mind but Zac had been so casual that he thought no more about it.

As his tutor had said, styles were changing fast in London. When Ben took a new canvas into the gallery, the director asked him if he had seen the latest American exhibition. Ben was excited.

'It's great, isn't it, these Abstract paintings! Not old-fashioned painterly stuff like Auerbach. It's painting with something new to say.'

The director looked at him in silence.

'You like the work I bring you, don't you?' Ben asked.

'You seem to be developing, I can see, but not in a way that is useful to us. We … the gallery has to keep up standards, nurture a certain style. We like painting, not old-fashioned of course, but pictures that people like to buy. Do you understand? See what you can do.'

But, as the weeks passed, Ben found more and more of his work rejected by the gallery until eventually he received a curt note from the director informing him that the gallery regretted that it could no longer represent him. He was sick with frustration; did this mean returning to the North and giving up London life? He poured out his rage to Zac, who told him to chill out and live, man. Without looking for another gallery, Ben took a job working in a pub; it kept him in touch with the art crowd and paid his rent.

One evening, walking up Cork Street, he found a Private View in progress at his old gallery. He walked in and avoiding the director, examined the paintings. They were very similar to his work but who was the artist? And then he saw the artist, surrounded by ladies who cooed and offered commissions and dinners. The receptionist looked embarrassed and tried to halt Ben but he pushed through the crowd of ladies and confronted Zac.

'What the hell are you doing here? This is my painting, you know it. You bloody well stepped into my shoes, you bloody plagiarist. Some friend!'

Zac shrugged his shoulders, and grinned.

'Hey, get a life …'

With a surge of rage, Ben punched him on the nose; the crowd fell away around him with loud gasps.

He found himself being man-handled to the door and heard a lady say, call the police and the director say, no don't bother, he's not worth the trouble. He stalked off and went to drink himself senseless.

The following evening, he went to the usual pub in Pimlico. Zac was near the door with a group of friends, celebrating noisily. Ben bought himself a drink and sat across the room. Zac looked at him; there was a large plaster on his nose and he had a black eye. Before he had finished his drink, Ben went over to him, ignoring his friends.

'I hope you are satisfied, you bastard. You've stolen my art and my gallery. I hope you're satisfied, you smarmy thieving bastard!' And poured the rest of his beer over him. Without waiting for a reaction, he left and walked down the road; he doubted that Zac had the bottle to follow and pick a fight. A moment later, there was a shout; Zac and two revellers were thundering down the pavement towards him. He took to his heels; it was the wisest course but he didn't go far enough. In Upper Bond Street, he ran out of breath and road and collapsed next to Churchill.

When he came out of hospital a month later, he found a job working in a new gallery, hanging pictures, talking to customers and preparing sales. He learnt to see the art world not as an outlet for poor young artists but as a market for selling to the rich and making a quick profit. He acquired the language and approach that the gallery required and his northern accent was deemed a cultural advantage, different from the Cockney accents becoming so common in the West End. After a year, the director of the gallery announced that he had purchased another gallery in the country and asked Ben whether he would be interested in managing the London gallery for him. A substantial pay rise came with the job and a percentage of all sales and he worked long hours, extracting the maximum sale prices while ensuring that the artists' share did not increase. By canny persuasion and a few hollow promises, he managed to keep the best artists and attract new ones.

One day, a young student from the North appeared at his office door. In one hand he held a reference from his old tutor and in the other a bundle of paintings and drawings. The student laid out the work, looking around at the gallery with awe. Ben smiled.

'Do you have any more of these?' he asked.

'Yes. Quite a few, … there are a few others that aren't finished yet …'

'When could you have them here?'

'Well, I don't know… do you want …'

'This style of yours is unusual; reminds me a bit of early Hockney. You know his work? Good. I think we could offer you an exhibition; would that interest you? Usual terms and if all goes well, we could talk about a contract.'

'Really? … When do you want to see the others?'

'Can you get them to me sometime next week? And, by the way, I appreciate that your garb matches your paintings but we prefer our artists a little more presentable. Let me loan you a hundred pounds; it'll come out of any sales. Get yourself some new clothes. Have a look around the gallery; you'll get the idea of what we like.'

A Summer's Day

'Look, look! The clouds are drawing back on all sides, like curtains on a stage.'

Except that stage curtains draw from two sides only and now the clouds were drawing back on all sides, puffy white clouds, bank on bank, drawing back to reveal

Blue.

The infinitesimal blue of space.

I didn't

I didn't like to say. Have you ever seen clouds draw apart on all sides? At the same time? What direction was the wind coming from? Was this what it was like being in the middle of a tornado? And yet, when I thought about it, where was the wind?

Still air.

I thought it had been a gentle south-westerly when I proposed a picnic on the Downs and we had climbed to the top of the hill and lay there on a rug, hand in hand, gazing into infinity. And the future. I don't know what she was thinking but I can remember my thoughts exactly.

But

then the clouds. All drawing apart at the same time, at the same pace. And no wind. It was as though we were looking up a round shaft through cloud, as high as Everest. Or higher.

She giggled. 'I'm so lucky, lucky, lucky … it's like a performance put on for us. The two of us.' She clutched my arm, planted a kiss on my cheek.

A contrail appeared, moving smoothly across the blue, from one side to the other. Too high to spot the sparkle of a plane. The contrail did not fade or drift, as they do, but remained a chalky white line. Drawn from side to side.

Another contrail appeared at right-angles to the first. Side to side. Not fading or drifting.

And then another … and another … until they were coming fast from all directions, lapping each other, knotting and pleating, knitting and weaving, until the sky was a dense pattern, lacelike, hardly a patch of blue to be seen.

She

'Isn't it wonderful? I've never seen the sky do this before.' A pause. 'What does it mean, do you think? Why are the Americans making patterns?'

Eh?

I didn't like to tell her that I didn't think it was the

Americans. Nor point out that the contrails were not like any contrail I had ever seen.

Now

the sky was becoming darker, as though the lacework was shutting out daylight. I sat up.

She ...

'Oh, don't let's go, darling ... it's marvellous ... isn't it? Say something!' A frown.

The clouds had descended to the ground, unnoticed, a dense curtain about a mile or so distant in all directions. I could see neither person nor animal nor any feature. Just the sheep shorn grass stretching in all directions.

Now

I stood, pulling on clothes, collecting food, drink, baskets and rug. She had risen, a little wobbly, looking around. It was colder. And there was a strange smell, metallic. Clutching my shoulder, she pulled on her shoes. High heels. Good for a country walk. I didn't think.

She

'What does it mean, Dave? I ... I don't like it. Anymore.'

We took the old path, beaten earth worn through the grass, down the hill to the village. We couldn't see the village. The village was hidden behind the cloud.

I wanted to run, but

we walked. And walked. She was panting a little. I was aware of the fabric of her clothes, a sleeveless cotton summer dress, brushing against my legs. I had never liked that dress.

The bank of cloud became no nearer and the village remained hidden. All we could see was the path, beaten earth worn through the grass, and dark cloud rising to a ceiling of white lacework. It seemed as if with each step we were advancing no further.

She

begged a rest, hanging on my arm. I looked around us and could see that the cloud was now rotating, spiralling upwards towards the top, not fast. It was darker. There was a humming, I hadn't noticed it before; a low bass sound like a choir of men trying to hum the same note and failing.

She

began a quiet sob, clutching my arm. 'Help me, Dave. Take me away from this. Please.'

As though I could.

It was very dark now; I couldn't see her. She hung onto me; began to scream. Swallowed it. We were hardly walking now, waiting ... waiting for what? She was crouching beside me, holding onto my legs.

I can't say when I was no longer on the ground. It was a curious floating sensation, drifting without sense of direction or distance, like a leaf caught in a stream. Where was I? Where was she for we had become separated though I could not remember her hands releasing me ...

Hmm

The humming had become louder, a more consistent note that drowned out any other sound there might have been: the wind, her cries, even the noise of my thoughts. I was aware of the humming as though I had become a radio transmitter tuned to no station, though to whom I was transmitting and what the message was I had no idea. I tried to think, to think of anything. Susie without clothes, what we ate for lunch, how we could … it was no use; no thought would appear. I felt as blank as a piece of paper, waiting for the writing to appear.

And then

the rotation began.

You would think, would you not, that if your body were rotated, you would know whether you were upside down or on your side or any other way. I knew only that my body was being rotated like a leaf in the air but I had lost all sense of up or down or sideways. I just knew it.

And still I had no thoughts outside the hum.

There was no change in the darkness and beyond; no thoughts I was aware of, no feelings at all. No feeling of exhaustion or hunger or thirst or pain. Or even discomfort.

And yet there was a feeling. I felt happy. As though there was no tomorrow nor yesterday, no demands nor questions …

I was in limbo.

But after that limbo, and it is difficult to think in terms of before and after when there is no sense of time, I could feel no more.

We were lying on the grass, side by side, as though we had been laid out by the undertaker but with our arms at our sides. Our clothes were piled on either side of us with our other belongings, a neat little pyramid beside each of us.

The sky was
Blue
puffy white clouds passing over.

The village was near, half a mile or so. People were going to and fro, the normal bustle of a working day.

She sat up with a shock.

'Oh, oh.' She started to scream, to scrabble among her clothes. 'Don't look, don't look … oh, how can you!'

We dressed. She was sobbing, muttering. I wanted to know what she had experienced. Had she heard the humming, had she been weightless? Was she happy? But it was no good, she would not speak of it.

Ever.

And that was just the beginning of the end.

The Garden Pavilion

I shall try to put it to you as I see it. And take you with me. Please don't make a noise, close your eyes and set aside your preconceptions.

There is a path, a path that should only be walked in one direction. A path of self-discovery and contemplation. But I am getting ahead of myself.

The path leaves the Hall by the Conservatory, as you would expect, and skirts the lawn to the arboretum. Mown grass, a flat ordered path, clipped plants. The house is away to one side, dominating, authoritarian. The arboretum is a controlled environment, labelled and documented, scientific. All is rational order. The path leads you rapidly away, into the shade of a wood.

An abrupt change; the path staggers, turns incomprehensible corners, circumnavigates slender trunks, holds you back in a darkness of confusion, deciduous and evergreen, that is never lifted. There are no bounds to the darkness but you have to go forward. At last, you see light at the end of the tunnel.

You look down. Stone slabs, irregular shapes, selected and cut so that they butt-joint each other, but on either side random, a jagged line which the grass and plants invade. A way that is not so regimented that you will be persuaded to pass along it at speed. Rather a path of opportunity, of decision, where you might wander rather than march, explore and learn.

Where it emerges from the trees, you see the land fall away, as you know it must eventually. But, before you can stop and gaze with relief at the gentle landscape, you are presented with an abrupt interruption; a building, the roof that swoops over you, a stone wall to one side of an opening, large boulders at the bottom reducing in size to the top where the roof projects. And on the other, a long timber wall, horizontal boarding leading the way over which the roof floats on a horizontal strip of glass.

The Pavilion.

The path takes you in. And shortly bridges a stream with a wide circular slab. The stream comes from our right, its channel formed from flattish boulders. It is not wide, not more than eighteen or twenty-four inches. To the left of the bridge, it departs the Pavilion and curves outside to run parallel to the path beyond.

Behind you the stone wall tumbles down and becomes the floor, green vegetation crawling up its surface. You look up but take care not to stumble; there is always the danger of a slip or a trip, and unexpected fall and ensuing damage. The front wall looks out over the valley, full height glass; a clear sheet with glass ribs doubled at either end, glass seats, glass shelves between with books, or rather slabs, of slate, stone, timber.

The Pavilion is not a place that I recommend you to recline, seek solace or delay beyond a passing interest. Not a place to take a book or make an assignation, but you will be tempted. It is a place of challenge for passing through at any speed that you might choose, a frame and conditioning to the world beyond: A river winding through the valley, two villages, church towers and a spire or two. A cultivated view, a destiny of reason. And a gentle rise of land beyond lifting into the hazy horizon. From where the sun shines at sunset, directly through the glass, a harsh warm illumination to break the cool lack of determination.

Should you dally here a while; there are small paths that lead from the bridge to the glass walls. You may be tempted to rest a short while on a glass seat; it will be cold, unyielding. Or you may wish to visit the 'library' and select a slab to feel. On either side of the paths are small boulders, grasses, mosses, low plants, mainly green. Look at them closely; you will not see their like in the park for they are of a distant landscape. Above you the roof; it appears to float like a disc over the walls as though there is no support. Polished steel on the underside, it reflects the light from all sides and if you look up you can look down on yourself; randomly on the path among the vegetation. At its centre is a large oval, open to the sky or closed; open to the interrogation of an open sky or closed by a screen that glows, the only source of artificial light.

And the path departs the building through the glass, a single polished timber post rising from the centre of the path.

It is a place to examine your thoughts and leave them. Perhaps a place for forgetting. It is certainly a place for the most essential of feelings. Hearing the wind moving through the trees and passing through the Pavilion. The sound of the stream tinkling over the stones. Smelling the damp green mosses. And perhaps the odd bright flower. Feeling the stone 'books', the oak and slate slabs. Viewing the framed and limited views of the world outside to which you hope to return. And tasting? Who knows?

You may not stay; it is too damp, or hard, or cold. Passing from the Pavilion, you continue down the path towards a pond, the stream accompanying you, a speedy private rushing; don't pause, don't hesitate, it says. The pond is a still dark water, a sink for unwanted things, standing adjacent to a mature stand of beech trees that curls away into the distant time.

Bid farewell to the view, bid farewell to the water, and rises uphill to the culmination of the walk, a place to be when thoughts are cleared and sunk, in stream and pond, a place to commune in relief.

Drowning

Early summer, a light overcast day, and John was running up to Orford under a southerly Force 3 over the early ebb tide. He was enjoying being alone; the clean shingle banks sliding past and terns fishing around him. Short of the quay, he rounded up, left the tiller and picked up a buoy. When he had dropped sail, checked the warp on the buoy and had a bite of lunch, he craved the company at the inn. The hard is muddy so he pulled on waders before drawing the dinghy alongside, dropped the oars into it, plucked the painter from the rail, and swung over the side.

At that moment, riding a swirl in the running tide, the dinghy swung out clear of the boat, like a puppy on a lead. And John descended without break into the river, the painter slipping from his grasp. He came up once, his waders filling with water, a brief gasp for air, and then his boots dragged him down. He came up once more, losing the battle, a desperate gasp.

A hand grasped his hair, not unkindly but firmly. And pulled him alongside a boat. His dinghy floated on unheeded, spinning lightly. With some assistance, he raised a leg over the rail, and was hauled without respect into the bottom of a cockpit, gushing water from boots and mouth. He gazed up at his rescuer and a young woman gazed down at him.

'Saw your dinghy go past. Good thing I did; wouldn't have come on deck otherwise. Come on, let's get your wet things off.'

And he was swept into the little cabin, where he stripped before the unabashed young sailor, rolled up in her bunk, and was fed hot soup. Shock set in, shaking and muddling. She was gone, hunting his dinghy. Later, much later, he stood on her deck, warm and dry, looking down at his dinghy. A brief hug and many thanks, and he went on his way, waders in the stern.

Early summer, a light overcast day in London. Celia is lunching with their publisher; John is happy to relinquish such tasks and go sailing. And she is happy to be lunched in Soho, a nice French meal with good wine and cheese. They have settled business without omission or delay before the entrée and are looking forward to 'lapin á la ...', and then a tarte tatin or perhaps a crepe suzette with half a bottle of Sauternes.

And she sits up abruptly. 'What time is it, Frank?'

'Why, it's half past one. Why do you want to know?'

'I must go. I don't know why. There is still time to catch the two thirty; I must go.' And away she goes without lapin or tarte.

Later that afternoon, she gets home and immediately looks for the reason that she has had to return. No burglar has invaded their home; the boiler is working and the car is in the garage. But upstairs, John lies in bed asleep.

'What are you doing here? I thought you were up the Alde.'

'I went in the river but somebody rescued me. I came back early.'

'In the river? How? When was that?'

'Oh, I don't know. My watch is on the chest-of-drawer; maybe …'

But she had already found it. 'Oh…It's stopped, full of water, at half past one.'

In Making Porridge

3.15a.m. I go for a pee, treading gently on the butt-jointed elm boards; uneven, adze marks, knots, repaired with care. Some creak; make note of those. An owl hoots from the trees, ash or oak or alder, loud and distracted. Happy hunting; where is its partner?

A recipe : a set of instructions, to lead towards a particular outcome. Late Middle English from Latin – receive! (first used as an instruction in medical prescriptions). From the Oxford Dictionary of English. As in 'First catch your hare', a recipe for jugged hare, Mrs. Beeton's Book of Household Management, 1859 – 60. Receipt – something received. A contract between two parties, one to go forward and one to receive. As the occasion calls.

Method the Third:
Get someone else to do it.

This is not a method.[1]

Method the Second:
 The Microwave.
This is not a method.[2]

A pheasant is calling; to my ears it sounds disconsolate, lonely. It is not the mating or shooting season, and the bird may be single, satisfied in food but not in partnership. Ducks have this problem; there are always too many males. A female scurries before a pair or three males, generally preferring one over the others but giving all the idea that they have a chance. The female is skilled in this game; it is instinctive, part of survival.

---

1   This is known as procurement, the easy obtaining of services, free or not. Related actions: servitude, staffing, subjugation.

2   The use of the microwave cooker bypasses the process of cooking. Cooking, like the partnerships of life, may involve more than one person; it requires care, consideration of others, an understanding of the ingredients, a gentle watching, and a dedication for concern for the outcome, the product, the development of experience. The microwave process is like/as speed dating, a simulacrum of the real thing. The outcome looks and possibly tastes near the real thing, but it lacks the indefinable smell of the real thing, the slow melding of the parts. It lacks the experience of the making. Therefore, I cannot accept it as a method.

Method the First:[3]

Ingredients:

Oats.[4][5] A large cooking spoon, heaped or flat according to requirement, for each person.

Water. Cold, fresh, in the proportions approximately of one part of oats to four parts of water.[6]

---

3   In essence, it is the marriage of two parts, tempered with heat. Ingredients may be added, and the outcome may vary from a fluid relationship, where the parts rotate, separate and come together on occasion, to a thick clinging closeness, a tough elastic bond.

4   It is a matter of taste what oats are chosen. I like to use a mixture of finely ground oats and organic jumbo oats, to provide a cream with a bite, an essential texture that removes the porridge from the bland smoothness of a commercial product. Life is never fulfilling, without a bit of bite, a slight grit to temper the smoothness.

5   Oats have a long history, in the formation of communities, and the formalisation of human coupling. It is said that wild oats, or the grain of extinct grasses, were picked, ground like nuts and roots and found to be good eating, as long as you spat out the grit from the quern stones. How they found the process of cooking the flour and learning of its habits and potential is unknown, but agriculture followed, with experiment, and the grains were slowly refined and improved. Such industry required the organisation of large numbers of workers in preparing the seed bed, broadcasting, watering and caring, harvesting, and storing the grain. And human seed also became domesticated. The stores were like/ as the swollen belly of a pregnant woman, a bounty to be produced at a later date. Food was no longer collected and consumed on the moment; a communal sharing of life ahead in time was planned and enjoyed, through organization and the domestic settlement of human couples.

6   I have attempted the speed the process by using hot water; the end result is hasty, poor. Time is needed to achieve a

A Saucepan[7], thick bottomed, preferably heavy and of a size that the mixed contents rise to half height.

A tool for stirring[8]. A spatula, spoon, spootle, porridger, stick …

Additional ingredients, if desired:

Salt, milk, sugar.

Place the oats in the pan, and add water. If possible, soak overnight[9].

An hour before the meal, place on a low heat, stirring occasionally.[10] The mixture may tend to stick to the bottom of the pan.

---

gentle melding [that word again].

7   Note the construction of the word. A saucier is a cook who makes sauces. A sauce is a cunning combination to enliven the consummation; note the alternative uses of the word 'sauce' used during the ages, particularly relating to human behaviour.

8   Stirring is a necessary and composite action; it not only involves the recombining of elements as they heat up together, but also must involve getting to the bottom of things, dragging up the deposits that wish to be concealed below the mass of well-combined material. So it is with all relationships.

9   It is common for many of these processes to involve maturing overnight. Whether it is the effect of the moon, or the healing silence, or simply the need to nest …

10 This is a matter of taste and dedication. My parents placed the mixture in the bottom oven of the AGA and left it to cook overnight while they nested. I start the cooking, and return to read in bed; it is a good time to read. And it is a sociable time.

Leave for about half an hour.[11]

After this time, the oats should have swollen, and the mixture should be simmering.[12]

At this point, I add a little milk,[13] a splash. It depends upon how liquid the porridge should be; some like it scarcely able to fall off the spoon, others a fluid mix that slips down the gullet. Stir vigorously.

Turn down the heat, and simmer for another half hour.[14]

Stir and serve.

The house stirs, a creaking of ancient floorboards, a lavatory flushes. The trees murmur in a growing breeze, and sunlight glows through the curtain. It is a time apart, when one rises as others slumber on; the hour for reading, a warm back pressed against one's side. Perhaps a wakening stirring. A car passes, a quick rushing sound. A blackbird gives an alarm call, strident and demanding.

---

11 Of course, this entirely depends upon the cooker, the thickness of the saucepan, the volume of the contents. Only experience can tell us how things may develop.

12 This is the word for the melding of the ingredients, and the development of something new. It suggests the gentle but irreversible change in relationships, the anticipation of a rich and fulfilling combination.

13 I use semi-skimmed; a full milk would give a richer mix. I haven't tried the alternatives, soya, almond, coconut. What sort of an exotic mix do you want, for goodness sake? Of course, some combinations are richer, international …

14 See note 11.

The meal[15]:

The Traditional Scot eats it with salt; I add a small amount of milk.

The pan may, or may not, have a crust on the bottom, a rubbery half-toasted layer that adheres to the pan. It is easily soaked and removed.[16]

Failure.

It is always possible[17]. A stout stir with the addition of a little hot water will recover most mixes, but if it has dried to a leathery composition, another use could be found for it. It may be laid in a pan to fully dry and fried in beef dripping or pork fat. A bannock or a barr? Perhaps a sledge. Or fed to the birds.

Then return to the top. Recommence associations, connections, and ingredients.

---

15 To be shared, an essential element. A coming-together of all ingredients and persons, a consummation. And in the consuming, a heat that radiates repletion, joy and fulfillment.

16 I have hopes one day of removing it, like a bannock; an oatcake of sorts. It has a colour to it, a faint biscuit, the crust of dispute over a hasty irresolution to end in a mature marriage, a conjunction of parts tested by fire, proved by time. The best relationships pass through such a test, rise to float above a possible sinking. There should be satisfaction in the surmounting, a golden aura.

17 To fail is golden, the very essence of experience, the knowledge of the upside and the downside. It provides the tools for going forth, one's breeks hardened to meet a new challenge, to venture afresh upon the maiden field.

Flight

The spoon spins lazily like an asteroid six feet above the table, before descending tip first onto the rim of the fruit bowl. A butterfly hovers and floats away in the sunlight. The bowl shatters in an explosion of ceramic shards. As Vanessa reaches to take an apple, David's hand covers hers, speckling with splinters of glaze that grow into bright drops of blood. James giggles.

An hour and a half earlier, Jane has finished laying the table outside on the patio. She has devised a simple menu, sufficient to satisfy the men's need for meat while not being too heavy for a warm day. She has had to give her apologies to the Church; she would not have had time to attend Holy Eucharist, where she looks after the little ones, singing songs, separating bickering siblings, mopping tears and wiping bottoms. She fears that Bernard and Jocelyn, who have taken her under their wing, have noticed her absence; they are expected any minute. Will they be happy with the company, the food, and everything? Will they want her to do more at the Church?

A robin alights on a bush, black eyes inspecting her. She looks over the table, moves a fork half an inch to the left, lines up the serviettes parallel with the knives, checks the exact position of the glasses and rotates a chair by five degrees. Two petals have fallen on the table; she removes them, looks round and tucks them into her bra. With a sob, she rushes indoors and returns with a vacuum cleaner and proceeds to vacuum the table, chairs and patio and then starts on the lawn, sticking strictly to the mown stripes. What does Jane think of? Is it plants, or the cooking, or her children? No, none of these. She cannot get an image of David out of her mind, standing white shanked by the bed that morning with a glistening willy that shrinks snail-like into repose; does it have to be like that? So messy and unnecessary.

In the lounge, David stands quite still, listening to the vacuum cleaner. The garden is already immaculate, like the house. He listens to his breathing, even and soft, his hands hanging by his sides. When did Jane become so particular? Sometimes, he is worried; it seems that she wishes to eradicate every living thing that interferes with her sense of order. When he first met her, all those years ago, she was fourteen, a light happy girl who was easy to fall in love with, a love unfettered by possessions or worries. She had appeared at school, new to the country as her parents had returned from service overseas, and she was keen to grasp every experience, keen to explore and be explored. But since marriage and children, she has become a different person; she has put away the inquisitive child and become something else, something dark and fearful. Marriage is a strange process, full of pitfalls and delusions; had he hoped for a life of lightness and warmth? How long will it be before he is exterminated, like the weeds and vermin, something untidy to be removed? His mind drifts away and he forgets the lunch, the guests shortly to arrive, and is lost in dreams of being in another place altogether.

Gravel crunches on the other side of the house. Jane pauses, listening for the doorbell, and wonders whether David will bring their guests through the kitchen or through the lounge as she has asked him. They are early, a sort of social crime. A bee hovers over the flowers by the door. She flicks an invisible mote of dust off her sleeve. It is time to make the Melba toast. She has not made it before but has seen it prepared on television; it didn't look easy. Before she reaches the house, David appears at the French doors to the lounge with a young couple. The woman wears a dark green silk dress and a Hermes scarf, her dark glasses on her head, and the man looks smart, casual in loafers and blazer. She glances down at her own tweed twinset and her false pearls, her mother's pride.

'Darling, Robert and Vanessa,' he says, and turning to the guests, 'what will you have to drink?'

He disappears into the kitchen without a glance at Jane who stares at them, clutching the hoover to her bosom.

'What a beautiful garden,' says Vanessa. She looks at the garden without expression, shading her eyes with her hand. 'We have a bit of land at the Hall; but I'm hopeless at this sort of thing. Those trees with the lovely leaves; what are they?'

'Hi, very kind of you to invite us over,' says Robert.

Jane smiles at them, a smile that does not reach her eyes. David returns with a tray, bottle and glasses, and passes round wine; Jane refuses, hovers and then snatches a glass, disappearing into the kitchen.

'Do you like gardening? Jane does all the gardening. Won't let me do a thing.'

'Know what you mean, old boy,' says Robert. 'Frankly, my time is too valuable for that sort of thing. Leave it all to Notley; he knows what to do.' He is confident, cock-sure. He knows he is important; he lives in the big house.

'But what are those trees with beautiful leaves?' says Vanessa. 'We must get some of those. They're sweet. The avenue at the Hall is all oaks. So dark and horrible. Couldn't we have a little arboretum, darling?'

She imagines her own little nursery of trees to talk to, care for and wash. She has read about the Victorian enthusiast who washed the trunks of his trees every week to eliminate fungal growth; she hopes for this same devotion.

'They're quince,' says David. 'Would you like to see the garden?'

Robert watches Vanessa follow David up the garden; he settles into a chair at the table, looks at his watch and yawns. He is hung over. His father insisted on playing the War Game last night and again he drew the Saxons to be destroyed by his father's Normans. His arm aches from holding his shield against his father's mace. And then they had to have the ceremonial battle wake with mead and brandy. And Vanessa was unusually demanding this morning, droit de seigneuresse, she calls it. A robin alights on the table, looks at him head on one side.

He smells cooking and feels hungry. He wonders why he accepted this invitation and when they are going to eat; he could have been at his friends' barbecue, snoozing in a deckchair. Gerry would have got pissed as an ape again, hanging off the diving board, and Clarissa could never hold her drink; would she have stripped off yet again? They were all getting a bit tired of that. It wasn't as if … He eases his groin. A motor mower starts a few gardens away, roaring and grunting. An older couple come round the side of the bungalow.

'Do you think we have the right house?' says the man.

'Don't be silly, darling. If we had rung at the door as I … oh, never mind.'

Robert stands up slowly to face them. They are like

his parents-in-law, smoothed by years of comfortable living, self-assured and well dressed, bland.

'Hullo. Can I offer you a drink?' And he pours two large glasses.

The man sits down, unbuttons his jacket, and stretches out. He looks large and complacent, a bear sunning itself.

'How do you do? I'm Bernard and that's Jocelyn,' he says, indicating his wife who is disappearing into the kitchen. 'I don't think we've met before.' A blackbird calls in alarm, and a cat sidles out of the hedge.

'Robert.'

'Do you live around here?'

'Yes. I met David in the pub, a small matter of pheasant feathers.'

'Ah.' He straightens his shirt.

'And you?'

'Oh, we're village. Met them at church; they haven't been here long, you know. Amazing what they've done with the garden, isn't it?'

And he takes a long drink, gazing at the slim figure of Vanessa, her silk dress shimmering like an exotic butterfly under the fruit trees. Ah, to be young again. Did Jocelyn shimmer in her youth? He can't remember. Although there was that time in Paris before they were married, something about a dancer and her dog, or was it a bottle of crème de menthe …

At the end of the garden, David and Vanessa stare at a small statue in silence. It depicts Venus, cast in concrete, spangled with yellow lichen. A dead squirrel is draped around its shoulders with its forepaws neatly crossed over the tail, like a fox fur.

A light plane flies over. Two sparrows chase each other out of the hedge.

'That's all there is to see, really,' says David, turning his back on the statue. He is not going to mention the squirrel; it is part of that untidy bundle of family secrets that threatens to come untied, spill out into the light, like a pack of fighting dogs. 'I expect you have a large garden; it must be nice to walk about, escape from things.'

He looks back at the little garden, immaculate with not a leaf or blade out of place, like his wardrobe, both managed by his wife. The familiar feelings of claustrophobia rise like bile. He sniffs.

Vanessa looks at him. She wonders about the squirrel and the vacuum cleaner. Though she does not know him, she feels an unexpected jolt of empathy; he seems different from Robert's other friends, more gentle and sensitive than them, rather like the boys who used to be at dancing classes. She feels strong for him, like a young chestnut, spreading its limbs to support and harbour.

'I love being outside,' she says. 'But I work at this school, you know. They have so many trees and I sit indoors all day looking out of the window. When I was little, school always seemed to be cold. So cold. Was your school like that? And we were forbidden to climb trees. It was all I wanted to do, climb trees.'

David looks at her, standing side on. There is something deeply attractive; is it the face, concealing hidden ambitions and frustrations, or the way she stands? He sees through the glasses and the scarf and the silk dress to a lean strength, bending to the winds of change and desire. Trees; he feels that he could come to understand. After all, they belong in the great world where man has limited domain, where the laws and rules are different and all communion is natural and free. He feels like stripping her of her polite exterior and enclosing her in his goose wings.

He says, 'I loved school because of the space outside. We were allowed to build bonfires and machines. But what I really wanted to do was fly …'

'Sometimes, I think … I should be happy to live in a tree, to care and look after it, be one with it.' Curious, the flying, she thinks. Much better to be grounded, as a tree. She could harbour him, a home and perhaps a lover …

'I wanted to fly from the tallest tower so I built my wings, real goose feathers with ash spars that fitted my arms, and—'

'My first boyfriend was killed by a tree but it was his own fault; he was always mocking them. He was running from a bull and climbed into a tree; it cast him off, the limb gave way and he broke his back falling and then the bull ran over him.'

David stares. A blackbird takes off, shrieking an alarm.

'My wings were confiscated and I wasn't allowed to fly, to be free like a bird.' And he imagines soaring over the Hall, Vanessa waving from the top of a tree.

'We are never free, are we?' Vanessa looks at David, who drops his eyes and falls into silence. She feels him slipping away, out of her grasp, taking flight, a huge misshapen bird, somehow angelic too, to save her, save the world.

'Oh, you're a good man; I can see you would never fly away,' she says, turning away. A bullock bellows in the distance. 'What bird is that? It's gone. So blue.'

'A bluetit, I think. Do you ever visit National Trust houses?' David says, taking her arm. 'Their gardens are magnificent at this time of year, full of birds. And trees. We could—'

She shrugs him off. 'Oh, I've been to all of them at some time or other. Mummy knew the families and we used to go there for balls and hunts and so on.' She recalls being forced into smart clothes and smart behaviour and how boring the boys were, and the time she escaped with another girl until they were discovered in the garages asleep, wrapped up together in the back seat of a Bentley.

They drift back to the table but neither of them wants to be there. Is this a fledgling romance, one that will take root like the quince and bear hard-won sweet-smelling fruit? Or will he remain caged, a pleasure bird for uxorial consumption?

Jane and Jocelyn emerge from the kitchen. Bernard

booms away, boasting of the village and its qualities; now he is the village elder taking newcomers under his wing. David wonders how long he will go on and when the last couple will arrive. And he thinks of being on a high place, his arms stretched wide, to catch the thermals, ready to soar above all of this …

'Are you ok, David?' Bernard is frowning at him.

David looks around and drops his arms. Silence falls and a thrush flies over.

Jane hovers behind David, who says, 'I don't know where the others are. Shall we start?'

Jane and Jocelyn disappear into the kitchen, returning with bowls of salmon paste and baskets of burnt Melba toast. David opens wine and sits at one end with Vanessa on his right and Jocelyn on his left. Robert sits down next to Jocelyn and talks of holidays in Italy, dropping Italian phrases and recipes as he compares the merits of alternative regions, telling improbable stories of boar hunts and feasts and advising on the best airports. Jocelyn watches him with a slight smile, fiddling with the large ceramic balls on her necklace and slipping a word in now and then; when allowed. She asks him how often he has been there and learns that it was only twice, to the same Tuscan village.

Jane sits at the other end, upright and small in her chair, an empty seat on her right, Bernard protecting her left side. Her hands are in her lap, tightly gripped. Why is it that her dresses never have the glamour of

Vanessa's? Why is the toast burnt? She thinks briefly of gardening. She has to stay on top of the vermin, especially the squirrels. She is perfecting her technique; she has discovered that really, it is not difficult to kill. At one time, it meant twisting their little throats, or simply cutting off their heads; she has always been careful to wipe the blood off the secateurs, to avoid rust. And questions. But it is much better now. Her latest catapult is terrific; she thinks of bigger prey. The man in the shop had told her how she should be careful, that it was as powerful as a gun. A bull's eye at fifteen yards. But she can't show it to David; he might get ideas.

'Delicious salmon, my dear,' says Bernard, taking a large mouthful and spraying toast crumbs. Vanessa pecks at a small helping, a brightly coloured bird at feeding time. There is a loud sound of gravel crunching and after some minutes the doorbell rings. David slips away and the table falls silent. Bernard coughs on a toast crumb and Jocelyn gives him a look as he washes it down with a gulp of wine. A lavatory flushes in the house and David appears with two people and makes introductions. The woman apologises for their late arrival and sits down at once on Jane's right next to Robert, who looks down at her loose Indian blouse and cotton trousers. The man stands grinning behind the one empty seat between Bernard and Vanessa, watching them and asks where he should sit. Jane points awkwardly to the chair without looking at him. He sits, pours himself a glass of wine and grins at her.

'Got stuck in the pub, arguing about the difference between a stoat and a weasel; do you know the difference?' He looks her up and down. 'I say, you didn't get the pearls out for us, did you? Why, if I'd known that it was a posh do, I would have had words with Liz, suggested she put a bra on.'

'James!' snaps his wife.

Jane coughs and David asks James if he has enough toast.

There is much conversation, full of lies and promises, hope and despair; it weaves a tapestry of fiction. The roast chicken has been served and consumed by everybody except Vanessa, who continues to peck at her food. David opens two more bottles of wine. James attempts to draw out Vanessa but she ignores him or gives brief answers to his questions and sips at a glass of Perrier water. Occasionally, David wants to open his heart to her and each time he finds that she is staring at him, consuming him with her eyes, so that he falls silent gazing at his plate. He is frustrated; something has slipped away, something indefinable and precious. He finds it hard to concentrate, to play the host to his guests, none of whom he knows well. He is not even sure if he likes them; except for Vanessa, perhaps.

Jocelyn looks down the table, to check Bernard's wine glass; it is full again. She signals to him to warn him of over-drinking but he either does not see her or ignores her. James notices and laughs. Jane sits in silence, listening to Bernard, avoiding any communication with James. Bernard looks across the table.

'Do you live in the village?' he asks Liz.

'No. And you?'

'Yes, just over the other side of the church. I think David and Jane will like living here, in spite of the bungalow.'

'You don't approve of bungalows?'

'It is a bit small for them, isn't it?'

'And do you like living here?'

'Of course, it's lovely, peaceful, just what a retired old man like me needs. Tell me, what do you do?'

'Do you mean, do I have a proper job? No, actually I don't. Do you think I should?' Liz looks at him, a slight smile playing at the corner of her mouth. She has a round face with her dark hair cut in a pageboy style, her eyes are grey blue.

'I don't think there's much call for my kind of work round here,' she says.

'What … what kind of work is that?'

'Oh, social work, of a sort.'

'Perhaps I should tell everyone where I found you,' says James, giggling. 'On the street. Now you know what sort of social work she was doing.'

Bernard's mouth drops open. Jane wonders what James meant and then realises, going red. She hates talk of this sort; it is all so smutty and terrible. She coughs. If they must talk, why can't it be about holidays and children and nice things like that? Like

Robert; he seems nice. Perhaps he would teach her to shoot.

Liz looks at James who is picking his nose. The same old things are surfacing. A little wine and he can't help himself. She wishes that she had thrown away that flowery shirt, bought when he was a slim youth. Poor James, he has never grown out of that image of himself as a 1960s hippy. He wasn't even born then. She wonders if he is going to get much worse. Still, it will distract Bernard from staring down her cleavage; in a moment, she might be tempted to slap him, rather hard.

There is a break in the conversation and Robert can be heard talking at length to Jocelyn.

'…And then in February, we go skiing with a group of friends. You know, just six or eight of us in a chalet or apartment; don't do any cooking of course because, well, we're on holiday aren't we? There's always a girl to do that sort of thing … no not France, we like to look for something a bit different. Used to go to Switzerland but it's getting a bit common so we tried Aspen, you know, Colorado.'

James looks up. 'So you ski, do you?'

Robert ignores him and asks Jocelyn where she is going this summer. She replies, 'Nowhere this year, I think. But what's Aspen like? Do you bump into film-stars?'

James turns to Vanessa. He is beginning to sag, slurring his words.

'Are you a terribly good skier?' he says.

Vanessa looks as though she had been struck. Why has she been put next to this perfectly horrible man? And he is drunk.

'I really don't see that that has anything to do with it!' she says, putting down her glass and turning to David.

'This is frightfully good chicken,' she says. 'Do you cook? It's so nice when a man cooks, don't you think?' David blushes and mutters.

Liz turns to Robert. 'Do you like Americans? Isn't that rather far for a week's skiing?'

Robert looks up lazily, a lion that is king of all he surveys.

'Oh, we don't go for a week, it's not worth it. At least a fortnight!'

Liz wonders why she is sitting next to this prat; how much longer is she going to put up with this supercilious, arrogant ...

'And I like Americans,' says Robert. 'You know, they get on with things, don't seem to be fettered with the same old boring restrictions that hold us back. Like unions. And strikes. And class.'

'But, for goodness' sake' says Liz. 'They are all mad, excessive fundamentalists who love guns, take over other countries, execute people, use as much oil per person as a hundred Africans, have an appalling educational system, and breed fat children. And they do have class, all based on money.'

Robert gives a high-pitched laugh, making the glasses tinkle. Liz picks up her fork and starts stabbing the table in front of her; she feels a righteous humming in her mind. David watches the discussion; he feels remote from it and cannot understand why people waste their time arguing about something that they can't change.

'You know, they know how to work,' Robert says, tapping the table in front of him.

Here we go again, thinks Vanessa. It is that damned one hundred and fifty percent speech; if I hear it again, I might scream. I have never seen him work more than fifty percent. She looks away down the garden, blinking.

'It is like the story about test pilots,' says Robert. 'I'd always wondered how they prepare for something on the limits of their experience. Apparently, the main problem is always that of time; the choice is very simple: eject or stay with the plane. And if you stay with the plane, you know what actions to take. Everything's quite simple, apart from one factor: time. You need time to assess the situation, time to put a list of actions into effect. So they practise everything to one hundred and fifty percent faster. Do you see? It's a fantastic way to get more out of the working day. And that's what the Americans do. I've trained myself to work and play at one hundred and fifty percent and be the best.'

Vanessa gazes at her husband, who mistakes it for adoration and preens himself.

'But they going to ruin the world, with their excessive growth and greed. How can you support them?' says Liz.

'Here she goes again,' says James. 'Loves to put the Americans down, and put the world to—'

Liz sits back in her chair and picks up her glass. 'Oh, shut up, James! Why are you such a drunken prick?'

James leaps up, tipping his chair over, staggers and leaning on the table, says to her, 'Why are you such a bitch? God, I work long hours to support us while you dawdle in a charity shop—'

'You are a bastard, James, aren't you? Born with a silver spoon in your mouth and you can't even get a decent job! So, you attack me! Well, at least I was bringing in a wage. Before you decided to move out here; not much work for me out here, is there?'

Jane looks from one to the other; she is astonished at the argument and, at the same time, wonders why she never has arguments with her own husband. They seem to pass like ships in the night, full of courtesies and restraint. She does not hear anything, withdrawing into her thoughts and the past. When she was little, she would retreat from her parents' arguments and curl up in the quiet dark space below the table. At first, she used to get frightened and pee, a small puddle on the parquet floor that her mother never noticed. But then she taught herself to shut out the world. She remembers the shiny red shoes she wore and how she used to polish them with her handkerchief and hum so that she couldn't hear the words flying like bullets over the table. Yes, she thinks, she would like to learn to shoot with a gun; she thinks she might be rather good at it. She hums quietly to herself.

Vanessa observes the argument rolling on, the usual accusations and denials, and wishes that they would both leave. James is a horrible bore, drunk and aggressive and Liz is probably quite nice but won't leave Robert alone. And that will make him intolerable this evening. Eventually, the words peter out as James's tongue fails him and Liz has the final word with a lazy smile.

'That's right! Turn on me to justify your angst, you poor little boy. Go on, why don't you start on my parents? Or my failure to provide a child?'

There is a moment's silence. The roar of a jet fighter reverberates between the houses and somewhere a dog barks. Robert laughs and runs his hand through his blond locks. Vanessa gazes at Liz first with horror and then puts her hand to her mouth, her eyes filling with tears. She wonders whether she will ever get pregnant; she is beginning to think that Robert is infertile. Liz looks embarrassed and takes a deep drink. Jane returns to the present moment and stops humming. James staggers, clutching the table.

Bernard rises and picks up the chair for James who has lost the use of his legs and subsides into it. Bernard pours him a large glass of water and James pours it over his head, shaking himself like a spaniel with drops spinning in all directions, sparkling in the sunshine. Vanessa looks appalled at the drops on her dress and dabs her face with a serviette. Jane freezes, staring at David. Robert laughs again and whispers something to Jocelyn but she pretends not to hear.

Liz ignores James and says, 'Anyway, thanks to your friends the Americans, we're in the front line.'

'What do you mean?' says Robert.

'The American base down the road. They keep practising for war, we hear them all the time and they do these raids into Iraq and Libya and goodness knows where else, using us as a base. So, when the terrorists get their act together, where do think they will hit first with their IUDs and home-made nuclear devices?'

'I think you mean IED, dear,' says Jocelyn.

'It'll never come to that,' says Robert with a tight smile. 'They're not clever enough and the Americans will wipe them out.'

'I wouldn't be so sure about that,' says Bernard. 'They seem pretty clever to me and not afraid to work hard for what they want. Look at all these corner shops that used to be run by British people; they have taken them over.'

'Oh, come darling,' says Jocelyn. 'I don't think the people running corner shops will want to bomb the Americans; they are doing very well. And Mr. Jusuf is such a nice man.'

'They are very good at concealing themselves in the local population. It will be old people next,' says Liz.

'What will?' says Bernard, his big face wrinkled in confusion.

'You see them all the time and I bet you don't think twice. Coach loads of old people out on an outing. How do you know that they're not terrorists coming to blow up American housing or schools or the airbase or something? It would be the easiest thing. Can you imagine body-searching old people?'

'Oh really, don't be disgusting,' says Robert, fiddling with his cutlery.

'Is it possible?' says Jocelyn. 'Darling, are we safe here?'

Bernard ignores her and continues to stare at Liz.

'Oh, come on,' says Robert. 'The Secret Service or MI5 or MI6 or whoever will find them out. They always do.' He sits back, a smug smile.

'You mean, like King's Cross?' says Jocelyn.

'I hadn't looked at it like that,' says Bernard.

'What can we do?' says Vanessa.

'Darling, shall we go on holiday? Australia or somewhere?' says Jocelyn.

'They say that they are expecting an attack any day,' says Liz. 'On the base. They could be disguised as milkmen or farm workers or … or old people. Anyway, it could happen right under our noses and we would just be pawns, pawns in the war against revolution …'

'I think you mean terrorism,' says Robert.

'Where did you hear about it?' asks Vanessa. 'It sounds terrible. Do you know the security problems we have at school? We have this child from a Middle East country and all the parents suspect him of being a mole. He's only five. Poor little boy.'

'Everybody round here has heard the rumours. We have to do something.' Liz looks so concerned, that Robert gives her a hug. She shrugs it off; after a short while. 'We have to do something. It wouldn't surprise me if there were terrorists embedded at the base poisoning the water. Why doesn't somebody do something?'

Jocelyn looks at Bernard and says, 'Darling, what can we do? Do you think we can do anything? Perhaps we should pray.'

Liz stands up, waving her arms about. 'You know Greenham Common? We'll do it like that. Who'll come with me? We'll camp at their base, show them that we care, show them up.'

'Oh, I don't know … 'says Vanessa.

'You're quite a gal, aren't you?' says Robert, gazing warmly at Liz.

'Bang, Bang!' says James, sliding down in his chair and taking cover.

David sits still. For a short time, he thinks about America and European airbases. He starts thinking about Vanessa. He closes his eyes.

James looks at Robert and mutters, 'what a prat.'

Robert leans over the table and fills James's wine glass so that it overflows. Jane turns pale and shrinks back into her chair. James balances his spoon on the edge of the table and flips the end. It flies into the air.

At the explosion of the fruit bowl, everybody but James stands up, David dripping blood; there is a mixture of shock and amusement on their faces.

Jane stands, looks at David, a long still look, and then briefly round the table. A robin comes close, picking up crumbs, and flies up into a tree. Poor Jane, she is struggling to do the right thing; should she leave quietly or scream as circumstances overcome her? Pushing her chair back in and folding her serviette neatly by her place, she walks into the house. David watches. Liz stares at James and follows Jane. Vanessa takes care of David, wrapping a serviette around his hand, and with an arm round his waist, takes him into the house through the French doors. Like good Scouts, Bernard and Jocelyn spring into action, gathering up the remains of the fruit bowl, rounding up the fruit, and carrying everything into the kitchen. A blackbird bursts out in a shout of alarm.

James lounges in his chair. Robert, the leader of men that he is, strides round the table and grabs James by the shoulders.

'You little bastard, you horrible little oik. I ought to punch your stupid face.'

'Hey, cool it you prat,' said James as he stands up, twisting round to face Robert. His speech is slurred and he sways on his feet. 'You make me sick, you and your skiing holidays and your private schools. I bet you drive a BMW, don't you?' He vomits down Robert's front and folds forward into a ball on his chair.

Robert looks down at him, grunts, and tips up the chair. James clutches at the table cloth and collapses onto the ground, the table, bottles and glasses falling around him with a tinkling and crashing. Robert stands over him. A blackbird takes off in alarm, a sharp repetitive call echoing around the garden. Above them, a pure contrail appears, heading towards Stanstead. The bees buzz. Robert shakes himself with disgust, scrubs at his shirt with a serviette and disappears into the house, calling for Vanessa.

'What a beautiful evening,' says Jocelyn. She sips tea.

Bernard is stretched out in a deckchair, asleep. There is no sign of the table or its contents; all has been swept up and cleared away.

'Jane and Liz are going to the American base,' she says. 'She has left the children to David; I expect he will manage.'

Vanessa sits upright in a chair, watching the fruit trees. She doubts that David will manage but she does not say anything. She seems to be waiting for something.

'Why don't you come and have supper with us?' says Jocelyn. 'I'm sure I could rustle up something.'

'That's frightfully kind of you but I can't,' says Vanessa.

'You mustn't worry, you know; Jane and David will get over it. I think James is rather difficult.'

Vanessa is not worrying. She is not thinking of Robert or the lunch. She is thinking of David. She is wondering whether he will ever be free.

Birds sing, calling to each other in the quiet of a late afternoon. A faint smell of lavender hangs in the air. Nearby, someone is lighting a barbecue, the smoke rising straight into the blue sky. James and Robert vanished a long time before, Robert wearing a shirt of David's, which was too tight. He has said that he will take James home but Vanessa suspects that the two men might seek some entertainment on the way.

Bernard snorts and rolls sideways, muttering in his sleep. Jocelyn sits in her deckchair, a slight heroic smile on her face, gazing into the distance. There is a noise behind them; Vanessa stands, turning to the house, and raises her arms, a look of wonder on her face. On the ridge of the bungalow stands David, his arms stretched, sheathed with white wings, like an angel's; he bends his knees and takes off towards Vanessa.

A barn owl appears flying low over the garden, turning its round face to stare at the three people below and the huge misshapen bird, soaring.

The Boat

You have been talking about it for so long; you have bored everyone to tears about the boat that you going to build, how you need advice and help, a design to build, and how you are going to set out on the open seas, leave all your commitments behind, wife and children, and have time to yourself.

So here are the instructions.

But first let us recall how we came to this day. You probably don't remember how you came to my university room, full of life, a bottle in hand, and departed not less than two hours later having drunk my port and with my fiancée on your arm, to 'show her the town while my boring brother writes his essays'. And how you ensnared my girl, my life, my hopes, and married her with the full approval of family and friends, me forgotten in the corner of a pew. But you believed that everyone loved you, supported you in your vain exploits, lent you money and still returned to lend you more. And your wife bore you patiently and four boys the while, all to be fed and educated. And now you must build a boat, in spite of all; to leave them.

This is what you must do then:

Firstly, find a broad tree; your fine oak by the drive should serve well. Fell it at the end of winter so the sap is low, and plank it, two inches thick, setting aside a good piece with a grown elbow for the keel. Leave to air dry for three years.

In the meantime, you must find planking, one inch pitchpine from Canada, knot-free and in long lengths. Those floorboards in your attic look just the thing.

As well, locate deck beams, decking of best mahogany, futtocks, scantlings, keelson, stem, transom, garboards, grown elbows, rubbing strakes, frames and floors; you will need all these, also every manner of fixings.

Equip yourself with tools: a table saw, bandsaw, fretsaw, tenon saw, crosscut saw, keyhole saw, and a handy everyday saw. A steamer for the scantlings and planking. Clamps, mallets, hammers, screwdrivers, brace and multiple bits. Expense? It's worth it, isn't it?

And then to start building; you must find a good piece of sheltered well-drained land. In front of the diningroom windows should serve very well. Build a cover for the construction, at least sixteen feet high, thirty long and twelve wide; you will need a separate secure place for tool storage, a shed for the saw bench, a shelter for the steamer.

And then proceed to construct: Lay down the keel, ensuring that it is level and true, and well supported. Set up the frames on the keel when you have assembled them, the deck beams, lead ballast, the stem, transom and keelson. Make sure that all is level and true; if not, start again. You find this hard work? But remember, it is your little ship, your means to sail away from wife and children.

After, plank it all in pitchpine, steaming and clamping as needs be. Of course it is hard; no, you may not find many people who care to help you. Your wife complains about the lack of light in the diningroom? Well, reassure her, as you usually do. Deck it in, lay in the cabin linings (yes, I know it would have been easier to do it before the deck was on, but you didn't have the timber for it. Did you? Oh.)

When the hull is complete, the rigging: masts, bowsprit, gun bronze fittings, blocks. Standing rigging, running rigging, a couple of winches, a heavy Admiralty anchor, and a plough. Oh, and a folding one for kedging off; you don't know what kedging off is? Never mind. Did you build in the mast foot? No? That is a problem; back to step two.

Paint the hull in any colour you choose; green and pink is very dashing, don't you think? It will certainly get plenty of looks from the yachting types. Oil the decks, paint the name in bold letters along the sides, and step the mast. It's in front of the bedroom window? A small price to pay for the golden future.

Then you must hire in a low-loader, crane, yard to launch, mooring, and kit the boat with sails, food, water, charts, lights, and perhaps a small outboard engine. You need to lay a road over the front lawn to get the low-loader in? What a pity, I expect the grass will grow back; but you'll have to fill the pond in.

And then the day arrives. What a celebration! You invite friends, comrades, sailors, and don't forget your family. Your wife obliges by breaking a bottle of cheap bubbly over the stem. And they all stand on the quay, to see you set sail, set out upon your voyage; it's your time now. How's the boat? She looks well, a bit odd, that pink cabin roof; personal taste, I suppose.

And then, a mile or three offshore, you are shouting and waving; yes, have a good voyage! Bye! But later you find water in the cabin. Did you remember to caulk the hull before painting it? I'm afraid that you are sinking. How about getting in the dinghy? You don't have one? Or flares or a radio?

Did I mention a life jacket?

Lighter than Air

Lighter than air, an amusing way to describe it. More like a shifting of space directly adjacent to his head. A small calibre rifle, probably. He took off his helmet. In the mess, they called it playing Russian Roulette. It was forbidden in the trenches at the Front. What did he care? Look around and see the bodies building up, Death riding its rampant path through friend and foe. What was the point in it all?

Again, that flutter; overhead this time. Was this sniper preferring not to hit him? Really, this was quite unsupportable. It was not what they were all there for; they were meant to kill each other, with hate or otherwise. And on such a beautiful day as this, the sun showing warm through the autumn clouds; was that a bird he heard?

Again.

The damned sniper was playing with him. He was tempted to stand on the parapet, bare his chest and shout 'You useless lot of louts, you boys from the barnyard, when are you coming to get us? Hein?'

A bullet to either side. Which way should he step, then? He stepped to the right, there on the firestep, and a bullet clipped his right shoulder. He stepped to the left, to a tug on the left.

Who was this man? He felt no inclination to shoot back. There was time for that. He would have liked to climb the parapet and walk the narrow line between the bullets, stumble through No Man's Land in a straight line until he could face this man. This joker.

And either punch him on the nose or share a Schnapps with him. He smiled and raised his hand in a salute. The bullet was neither right nor left nor too high.

That evening, the Kolonel raised his glass. 'A toast. Bad luck, Lt Schimmer. Now, gentlemen, who's for cards?'

The Saga of Geir Wolfströrm

1

There was a man named Ketil Broken-Hall. He was a mighty man who lived in the North of Norway. He was the son of Thorhild Aranson The Learned who was the son of Hallstein the Godi, the son of Giant-Bjorn. At that time, King Harald Fair-Hair grew so powerful that no man could thrive in Norway unless he had paid his dues to the throne. So Ketil Broken-Hall bought a ship which was beached at Hrafnista and sailed with rich goods to Iceland. It was a good journey and they landed in the West in Hvammsfjord. They were made welcome and he and his men stayed there. However there was no land that he could call his own so after fourteen days feasting and bearing splendid gifts, they bid farewell to their cousins and sailed to the North to Vatnafjord where they were made welcome and Ketil built a large hall with two farms and became a powerful and influential man in those parts.

2

The story now turns to his descendants. Many generations have passed and the family now has the name of Wolfströrm. And there were Geir and Hruf and many other cousins who do not form a part in this tale. Geir was a very strong man, proud and well dressed, sometimes quick to anger; his neighbours had respect for him but he was not much liked. He owned farms and a factory that made electronic components. He was good with both his hands and mind, always designing improvements. His cousin Hruf was also a farmer; he did not thrive and his farm was poor but he was a poet and much loved by the people around and welcome in many homesteads.

Now there was a man called Thorgrim, who was a very proud man with a small farm and he had a daughter of twenty summers who was very beautiful and clever. Her name was Gudrun. Hruf had wooed Gudrun for some years; it was not possible to arrange the marriage because Hruf did not have sufficient wealth to build a good homestead and satisfy the honour of Thorgrim the father of Gudrun. But Gudrun loved Hruf and would look at no other man. One day, Geir went to Thorgrim and offered him a large sum of money, gold rings and a silk cloak, to persuade Gudrun to marry him. And Thorgrim said that if he settled half the wealth of his farms on Gudrun, he would speak to her and persuade her to marry Geir.

When the matter was put to Gudrun, she wept

for she loved Hruf but she did not wish to disobey her father. Thorgrim told her that she would have much wealth and a good home. So the marriage was arranged and there was a great feast at Geir's hall with two thousand guests that lasted for three days. But Geir and Gudrun did not have a good marriage because Gudrun loved another and Geir was always busy and often away from the hall. Hruf was very unhappy and spoke to Thorgrim but Thorgrim was glad to have Gudrun make a wealthy marriage and told Hruf to go away. So Hruf took his complaint to the Althing and went to the booth of Bjork Kjallakson, a good man, a lawyer and a friend and supporter of the Wolfströrm family. Bjork listened to him with great patience and tried to persuade Hruf from starting a feud; he said that he would approach Geir and ask him to pay compensation for the ill that he had caused Hruf. But Hruf grew angry, and weeping violently, left the booth.

3

I must tell you that this was at the time of the great Fuel Famine. The rich countries in the world had used all their oil and had for many years bought oil from the desert countries. But the desert countries had used almost all their oil and kept the rest for themselves. The poor countries had suffered a great starvation with many millions dying and the rich countries without oil had had to build new technologies to make life possible; there was very little trading and many countries lived in fear of each other. But after a time, they realised that there was little to be gained by war and slowly life was improving. The poor countries grew bio-fuels to trade to the rich countries for medicines and electronic goods and the rich countries developed more technologies. For some time, no countries had thought about space travel but with the growth in micro-electronic technologies, there came the need to establish satellites around the world and a search in space for minerals. At this time, there was much discussion but nobody had been able to think of a scheme that would be economical and effective.

However, Geir had brought together designers and engineers and he had an idea. He called it the Space Elevator. The great expense and use of energy in space travel, he knew, was in escaping the Earth's gravity and atmosphere. Geir had been consumed by this problem and his idea was quite simple and clever.

He would build a tube about 90 miles long, rising into the sky to the limits of the atmosphere where gravity is much less. Capsules would run within this tube to carry goods and personnel up to a Space Station located on the edge of the Earth's atmosphere. After all, he said, 90 miles is not so long if one considers the length of railway lines, tunnels through mountains and under seas, and pipelines laid across the oceans. Of course, this Tube could not stand on the land for the foundations would be too great. The Space Elevator would be self-supporting and navigable, automatically sited by satellite location devices as are deep sea drilling rigs, and flexible enough to allow for storms, wind changes, jet-stream variations and pressure fluctuations. It would have balloons and multi-rotating boosters to supply lift and location in a geo-stationary location. His electronics firm would supply all the management and technical equipment and he would establish a business to construct the Space Elevator, passing control onto an organisation composed of powers from different countries. He would take the charge and profit from each 'scend'; that is, each journey of the capsule a-scending and de-scending.

The location of the Space Elevator was very important; there were a large number of considerations. It would have to be in a politically stable country. It would have to be where there was a source of energy for 'flying' the Elevator. It would have to be near the countries that would have an interest in using it. It would have to be constructed of easily available material, purchased at a moderate cost. And it would have to be located where any collapse or explosion would not cause damage or injury. So he looked at the Eastern part of Iceland. There were many advantages and some disadvantages: There were no ports and few roads. There was a risk of seismic movement. The weather was often inclement, deep snow, rain and cold. However, there were no other businesses, very light human habitation and farming, and most important of all, there was a plentiful supply of energy to be freely harnessed, hydro-electric from rivers and the sea, hot gases and water from beneath the ground. And if the ground should move, as in Japan and Iceland so many times before, the Space Elevator would have a light foot upon the ground and could be 'flown' out of trouble. And should a collapse occur, it would fall upon uninhabited land and the sea.

So he persuaded the Government of Iceland to build new roads to the East and he started construction of the base and Elevator on land North of Hrafnkelsstadir. For the Tube, he purchased many redundant aircraft fuselages which are built for lightness and stiffness against the stresses of air pressure, constructed connectors out of carbon-fibre and capsules from aircraft and space parts. It grew from the ground upwards, section by section, hoisted by balloons and its own engines. At the base, it rose at 30° to the horizontal, becoming more vertical the higher it went until it disappeared above the frequently low clouds into the blue space above. The construction of the top section was more difficult; but they established a workstation at 50 miles up and projected the growing top section upwards from there, using balloons and small jets powered by the methane piped from beneath the ground. They found that the journey into space took 100 minutes and the station at the top was quite stable, suitable for launching light rockets carrying satellites and space-ships.

This great work took some time but less than many would have imagined and the Elevator was opened by the President of Iceland with a great feast with important people of many countries present and free rides offered to the Space Station where they could enjoy weightlessness and cocktails. And before long, there was a line of customers, all wishing to have access to space, some for exploration, some for tourism (round world trips offered), some for space laboratories, and most for satellite location, both commercial and military. And Geir began to work on his new scheme for constructing and locating a sun-reflecting satellite, fifty miles across, to provide power on Earth. But that is another story.

4

That same year that the Elevator was completed, Geir was well rewarded and bemedalled by many countries who saw that good would come of his enterprise and he became rich and powerful. But Gudrun stayed on the farm and hardly saw him at all, not even for begetting a child, and she became sad and unhappy. She wished to divorce Geir but her father Thorgrim was still alive and Geir's importance reflected on him and he became boastful and self-important so that his neighbours no longer knew him. He would not consider any wish of Gudrun to start divorce proceedings. Hruf saw all of this and was angry. He visited Gudrun when he knew that Thorgrim was away on business and saw how unhappy she had become. She would not listen to any schemes for revenge and implored him to travel to find a new life in some other land. But he would not accept her offer of money and went back to his farm.

At night, he had dreams. Sometimes it was the good-dream woman who showed him a life on the farm with Gudrun and sometimes it was the bad dream-woman who showed him death of a man. He was consumed with revenge against his cousin Geir and called upon eleven friends to come with him and seek satisfaction. He feasted them well and spoke this verse:

> Geir has robbed
> Me of much.
> I lacked the might
> To seek justice against
> the killer of my dreams.
> Myself I know
> That I have the makings
> Of a worthy man,
> Who seeks justice.
> Where the winds of the
> moon-bear rages,
> shall we rage the battle.

The next day at nightfall, they rode out of the farm with bedrolls and food for they did not plan to stay at any farm on the way. Two days later, they camped in the mountains above the Elevator base and Hruf made plans to carry out the revenge on Geir. His friends warned him that he would be outlawed and that nobody could help him escape the country; but Hruf felt that he would lose honour if he withdrew and told his men that they should have no part in the revenge.

At dawn, they rode down to the base and under cover of a thick cloud, laid explosives around the base of the Elevator. Then Hruf approached the guards and asked them where he could find Geir; the guards were suspicious and wanted to lay arms upon him and hand him over to the police but Hruf told them that Geir was his close cousin and had invited him to ride to space with him. Then the guards told Hruf that Geir was at Space Station and that he would have to return at another time and they were relieved to see him go because they had felt uneasy in his presence. Hruf rejoined his men under the cover of cloud and he rejoiced. Then they set off the explosive charges.

At first, there was nothing to be seen; only a dull rumble broke the peace. And then sirens started and there was a great noise of breaking and rending with explosions of gas, flashes of broken electrical lines, flowing water and gas-oil. Hruf and his men did not know what would happen; they had thought only of damaging the base. But in front of their eyes, the Elevator started to rise into the sky, bumping along the ground with all the gas and electricity and gas-oil pipes and communication lines trailing behind. They were silent in awe and terror at what they had done and the eleven men mounted up and rode away fast leaving Hruf standing alone. They had a harsh journey with much travail before they reached their homes but that is another tale. After a time, the dust settled and the cloud lifted and there was a great scar across the land. But Hruf had gone, riding across the great wastes of the North by himself, camping in the lee of cliffs and wondering where to go.

On the Space Elevator, all the life support systems broke and emergency back-ups brought oxygen and light to Geir and the men and women working at Space Station. The Elevator floated over the sea, bouncing on the waves but keeping upright. Geir spoke over the e-plate to a number of airmen and before long, there were American helicopters working to halt the movement and bring the Elevator to land. They anchored it over the Faroes and waited for friendly winds before flying back to Iceland; in the meantime, repairs were carried out at the base and a new platform installed. Hruf had not caused as much damage as he had wished.

Hruf returned to Gudrun and said that he had killed Geir by causing the Elevator to break away. Silently, Gudrun took him to the e-plate and there he saw Geir, directing operations calmly from the mid-station. And then Geir turned and spoke to him, not angrily or unkindly though he had caused much damage. And Hruf was full of sadness and going to the coast, took a small boat and set out upon the sea and was not seen again. And Gudrun, despairing of Geir and her life, left her hall one night and settled on a life of sacrifice, moving from farm to farm helping aged and poor farmers in the house and in the cowshed until she died of exhaustion. Here ends the saga.